Gift

of the

Concordia

Faculty Women

A Spirit
to Ride the
Whirlwind

A Spirit to Ride the Whirlwind

By Athena V. Lord

MACMILLAN PUBLISHING CO., INC.
New York
COLLIER MACMILLAN PUBLISHERS
London

Macmillan Publishing Co., Inc.
866 Third Avenue, New York, N.Y. 10022
Collier Macmillan Canada, Ltd.
Printed in the United States of America

10 9 8 7 6 5 4 3 2 1

LIBRARY OF CONGRESS CATALOGING IN PUBLICATION DATA
Lord, Athena V.
   A spirit to ride the whirlwind.
   SUMMARY: Twelve-year-old Binnie, whose mother runs
a company boarding house in Lowell, Massachusetts,
begins working in a textile mill and is caught up in
the 1836 strike of women workers.
   [1. Women—Employment—Fiction.   2. Lodging
houses—Fiction.   3. Children—Employment—Fiction.
4. Strikes and lockouts—Fiction.   5. Industry—
History—Fiction]   I. Title.
PZ7.L8769Sp   [Fic]   81-3775   ISBN 0-02-761410-7   AACR2

THIS BOOK IS DEDICATED TO ATHANASIUS T. VAVURAS AND
ARALUKA KERAMARI VAVURAS, WHOSE RESTAURANT IN
COHOES, NEW YORK, ONE HUNDRED YEARS LATER
PROVIDED GOOD FOOD AND SPIRITUAL EMPATHY
FOR THE MILLWORKERS ON THE HILL

A Spirit
to Ride the
Whirlwind

1

How-how, who-who. Howe-Howe. Arabinia Howe. Why-why. 'Cause she's gonna cry. Why-why. 'Cause she's gonna die.

Hunkering down into the collar of her cloak, Arabinia Howe felt she had good reason to cry and thought it quite likely that she would die. It would serve her mother right for making her go out in the pouring rain. Blown by the gusting winds, sheets of rain slashed with a cutting edge against her face, drizzled down in every opening of her cloak and whipped her long skirt into a binding rope around her ankles. She struggled to walk faster.

Inky-stinky. Inky-stinky blackness.

There wasn't a sliver of light from the heavens above to break the darkness. She placed each foot with a blind hope and prayer that it would land on the mucky path. She thought of Christian who had journeyed through The Valley of Death in *Pilgrim's Progress*. He—though suffering—had had his path lit by the flames of Hell, she remembered. And the flames must have warmed him as well. She shivered again. Anger made her move more quickly still.

How-how, why-why. 'Cause she's gonna cry. When-when. At half-past ten. Her mind played with the rhymes and her feet moved to keep time with the words.

Smash. The right foot placed too high had banged into a hard, solid tree trunk, stubbing all five toes at once. Arabinia

Howe yelped and cursed: Ye gods and little fishes! There was no one to hear and no one to wipe her tears. Nor could she do anything for herself. Clutching the dinner pail under her cloak, she didn't even have a hand free to rub her aching foot.

At least the stubbing had told her where she was. The big elm marked the point at which the path to the Print Works branched off. As she turned left, Binnie could recall her mother's voice from the doorway sending her off.

"You'll need to keep the pail dry under your cloak. No sense taking the umbrella. The wind will only tear it inside out. Hurry, Binnie, hurry."

Nothing would convince Mama that a later start might be better; that perhaps the errand could wait until the rain let up or the wind died down.

"We have an Obligation, Binnie. We must honor our agreement to give Mr. Pratt his supper." Mama's voice spelled the word *Obligation* with a capital *O* and made it sound like one of the Ten Commandments.

Strange, thought Binnie, how Mama could change age around to suit her needs. For Obligations, she insisted that a girl almost twelve was full-grown, too big to be excused from work for play. Yet when Binnie asked for a gold breast-pin to wear on her dress, Mama said "little-girls-just-eleven" had no business asking for the trimmings of a lady's dress.

If another tree had appeared just then, an angry Binnie would have kicked it happily. A dim flickering light ahead promised that the end of this trip was in sight. Binnie skittered to a halt in the slippery mud by the Print Works gates. With a cold, wet hand, she reached down inside her cloak to find the tin whistle that Mama had hung around her neck.

Blowing hard, shrill blasts on the whistle, she watched and waited for the light to move. Would Mr. Pratt, the night watchman, hear her signal over the whistling wind and loud drumming rain? Where was Mr. Pratt? Why didn't the light bob out of the door to the gate where she waited?

In a sudden panic, Binnie blew the whistle again and again. She never heard a voice, only felt the hand grabbing at her shoulder. Through the open filligree of the iron gates, she saw a darker solid blob. He must have come without a light.

"Here! Here! Give me the pail, girl," he commanded.

Crreak. Bang. The gates opened and shut. The pail was gone, the dark blob was gone and a shivering Binnie stood alone again in the black night.

Not even a please or a thank-you, she thought indignantly. How Mama would have scolded her for behaving so rudely. Binnie sniffed up. It was no use trying to wipe her nose; too much rain was pouring down. The soaked, muddy edges of her skirt hung like dead weights. Annoyed, she twitched and pulled the skirt away from her ankles as she turned herself around.

Now the gusting winds puffed against her back and hurried her steps instead of hindering them. Binnie's short, skinny legs pumped faster and faster. She felt like a schooner being blown off course and giggled at the thought. Wouldn't it be nice, though, if she could sail along above the mud? From the corner of her eye she saw a blue-white streak of lightning dance down toward the river and clapped her hands against her ears to muffle the bang of thunder that followed it. She heard the hollow sound of her own voice giving a soft moan. To watch lightning and hear thunder from the safety of the parlor window was one thing; to be outside exposed to its killing properties was another.

The only defense that she could think of was to jog faster yet. A moving target might be harder to hit and increasing her speed would surely bring her home much sooner.

At the same time, Binnie started singing as loudly as she could. It was, she told herself, a practical thing to do. If anyone else was out on the path, he would hear her coming and move out of the way. Binnie hardly dared to think who else might be out on such a night. With an effort, she pushed thoughts of robbers and Indians out of her mind. She concentrated instead on the next lines of "Barbara Allen":

> Go take this letter to my old true love and
> tell her I am dying . . . .

For such a small girl, her voice was surprisingly deep and powerful.

> She took the letter in her lily-white hand,
> she read it slow and moving . . . .

Binnie gasped. Her left foot was sliding down, down, without pause.

"Oh, dear God in Heaven," Binnie prayed. "Don't let me be near the canal. Don't let me be so far off the path."

Alice Howe, like every mother in Lowell, Massachusetts, daily warned her children not to play near the canals that laced the land between the Merrimack and the Concord rivers. The network of canals supplied water and power to the mills lining the riverbanks. Useful, pretty . . . and dangerous were the canals of Lowell in 1836.

Every so often, somebody fell in and got pulled out too

late. Binnie herself had seen the last one. Edging around the crowd, she had eyed with horrified fascination the lump covered by a gray homespun blanket. Whispers said it was a Paddy, one of the Irish who had come by the hundreds to dig still more canals for the ever-growing mills.

One especially ugly whisper had chanted, "Paddy Whacker, chew tobacker/If he dies, it is no matter."

She did not want to drown. Her mind leaped wildly as she tried to find a bargain that would please God.

"Oh, God, I promise . . . I promise never to take your name in vain. Never to be mean to little Aleck . . . ."

Her legs spread still more and the slippery mud brought her down in a painful split. She realized suddenly that it was not a canal. It was just a boggy hole that she had stepped into. Hands down in the mud, Binnie pushed herself back upright.

She shook herself like a wet dog from one end to the other and then gave her hands an extra shake. Through tears and rain, she spied a glimmer of light, something like the glow from the tail of a June bug. But it was a cold April, too early for the bugs. The pin-sized light multiplied into many, all spaced a house width apart. Home and safety were in sight.

"Say boo to Binnie and see how she runs," Adam, her older brother, had teased more than once. He meant it as a kind of compliment. As big as her brother was, he had to run hard to beat her. A scared, soaked Binnie ran faster now than ever.

Pounding down the path, she felt phrases popping like firecrackers in her head. Too much. Too much. Mama asked too much of a girl. No matter what the chore was, she never

7

asked the boys. Adam at sixteen was always too old, Aleck at five, too little. It wasn't fair. She would tell Mama how unfair . . . unjust . . . .

When she finally reached the door, Binnie banged hard for Mama to let her in. The corporation required all the boarding house women to keep their doors locked after curfew time. Women lodgers had to finish their visiting, their shopping or their evening school classes before ten P.M. The widow Howe, a constant worrier, always put the latch on early.

Binnie tumbled into the warm kitchen looking like a dirty curled-up leaf blown in by the wind. Whatever words she had meant to say, she had no breath left to shape them. Mama looked, picked up the hearth broom, and handed it to her.

"Brush yourself down by the door, Binnie, and then sweep that mud out quickly." Moving briskly, Mrs. Howe turned away and picked up the kettle of hot water.

As Binnie swept down the front of herself, she made no attempt to hide her tears. One little sob after another could be heard plainly; in fact, she raised her voice to make the sobs louder still. Mama, who was pouring the steaming water into a basin, paid no attention.

"Get your clothes off quickly before those wet things give you the grippe. Quickly."

Mama's favorite word was *quickly*. Everything had to be done faster than you could say "yesterday." Binnie's cold fingers could not unbutton speedily enough to suit Mama. In a minute, Mrs. Howe had stripped Binnie down to her flannel chemise, wrapped the old quilt around her shoulders and sat her down with feet planted in the mustard bath.

8

Tea, toast, cabbage and candle wax—the familiar kitchen smells mingled and were covered by the sharp prickly smell of mustard. Binnie could not decide whether to be angry or relieved. She had wanted so much to have her tears noticed and wiped away, to be petted and patted. She had wanted even to be hauled up on Mama's lap the way she had been years ago. On the other hand, the stingingly hot footbath felt good and soothing. And it was exactly what Mama offered the mill women for comfort.

"If I had the choice . . . send a child . . . ." Mama's voice rose. "You'd better have a mustard gargle, too." Her voice dropped to a mumble. ". . . if money . . . ." Mama talking to herself sounded the way she did when scolding Binnie. Only why, a puzzled Binnie wondered, was she so vexed with herself? A boarding house keeper had few enough ways to make extra money. And Mr. Pratt paid good hard silver for the meat, cheese, bread and jam that Mama sent him.

A figure appeared in the doorway from the dining room. "Mrs. Howe, I've come to . . . ."

"If it's hot water, you can see I've used it." Mama interrupted the speaker and nodded toward Binnie. "The girl has been out in this dirty weather carrying supper to the night watchman at the Print Works."

"No, no. My sister Grace has the toothache. I wondered . . . could you heat a soapstone . . . and . . . ."

Phoebe Little's ladylike voice faded away as her glance flicked over Binnie. "This dreadful downpour. . . . Do you suppose that the bells will ring tomorrow? And . . . ."

Her hands were fluttering like someone begging a favor, but she had the confident air of one who expects and deserves every attention. "She would so love to have you sit with her. Perhaps, too, a cup of camomile tea for her nerves if you should boil some water? I'll be upstairs with poor Grace."

Without waiting for an answer, Phoebe Little turned to leave. Her tall shadow was swallowed abruptly by the dark doorway.

"There's one who believes in getting her money's worth of service from the landlady," Mrs. Howe observed wryly. "Hop yourself into bed, Binnie. Why I have to play nurse to Grace when she has her own sister, Phoebe, right here . . . !" Mrs. Howe shrugged. From her apron pocket she took a small piece of barley sugar. "Suck on this to clear out any phlegm."

"Oh-hhh." Binnie popped it into her mouth and hurried to dry her feet on the hopsacking towel. She headed for the room off the kitchen and pushed aside the curtain that hung in the doorway. Aleck was already asleep in the trundle bed. Binnie raced now to get into her nightgown and jumped into the big double bed still fastening the top button. There. She had made it before Mama remembered about the mustard gargle.

"Mama," she called out, "thank you." Courtesies paid, Binnie pulled her head down under the covers. She pulled her knees up high against her chest, crossed her arms and tucked cold hands into her armpits to warm them. She began to breathe heavily, blowing warm air out around her balled-up body. "Lordwatchoverusall." On a single, long-exhaled breath, she finished her prayers. Dimly through the covers, she heard wisps of Mama's voice.

". . . elcome . . . morn . . . Honey."

Binnie's mind got caught on the last word and she forgot

to blow the next breath out. Way down in the cloudy memories of being a little girl younger than Aleck was now, she still held clearly the sound of Papa's voice saying that word. Honey.

Binnie used to plunk herself on Papa's crossed legs and he, lifting one foot, would swing her gently up and down. He called it a "horsey" ride for his "Honey-bunny Binnie." But Papa had been dead for ages and it was not Mama's way as a rule to use sweet words or pet names. Curiously, to hear herself called Honey now made Binnie feel grown-up.

Binnie pulled her head out cautiously from her dark cave. Now she could hear again the rain blowing past the house and drumming into the ground. This storm would send still more water into the rivers already swollen by melted snow from the highlands north of Lowell. Too much water would swamp the huge wooden water wheels that powered the drive shafts and pulleys in the mills. If those wheels didn't turn, there would be no way to move the carding machines, the spinning machines and the looms that wove cloth. The picture of fat rivers reminded her and she called out again:

"Will the bells ring tomorrow, Mama?"

"Binnie, how should I know what will happen tomorrow? I'm neither an agent nor an overseer. If you awaken Aleck, I'll . . . . Go to sleep, do you hear?" her mother commanded sharply. "You'll hear soon enough if the bells don't ring."

Like a turtle pulling into its shell, Binnie slowly rolled her head back under the covers and sighed. Her questions so often went unanswered. As she fell asleep, she was still puzzling over the answer to one last question. How could you *hear* something that wasn't going to ring? Wasn't it foolish to say the silence would wake you up?

Mornings, Mama got up long before any bells rang. She went around the house pulling back the inside shutters from the windows and starting up the fires in both the front room and the kitchen. Sometimes she had the kettle steaming before she remembered to call Binnie.

On those lucky days, Binnie sneaked a little time for herself. Scrambling out of bed, she would grab her clothes off the peg and then a book. Her dress she slid under the covers to be warmed in the hollow where she had lain. Her cloak, though scratchy and cold, she wrapped around herself. Hunched under the window, she would read by the first fingers of daylight filtering through the muslin curtains. She read until Mama called her or until Aleck woke up.

Opening one eye, Binnie could tell that this morning was not a lucky one. Although the tall wardrobe loomed bulky and indistinct, she could clearly make out the red fleur-de-lis painted on the pine blanket chest. Daylight was well on its way. Besides, she had nothing new to read and her cloak, still drying, hung out in the kitchen. To be awake, warm and idle was a rare state for Binnie. She pushed her legs straight down in a long, lazy stretch and relished the good feeling of not having a single thing to do. Her mind pushed back to her thoughts of the night before and she smiled to herself. The silence had not awakened her. So, she reasoned, the first bells must have rung as usual.

By April, the mills had already changed to the summer schedule. The gates opened with the first bells ringing at five o'clock so that the women put in a good two hours of work before returning home for breakfast. Those bells commanding them to work or dismissing them were very seldom stilled. Only two events could close all of the mills at one time and silence the bells completely: when spring rains swelled the rivers and feeder canals, upsetting the system of water distribution, and—more rarely still—when the calendar reached one of the few holidays recognized officially by the mill owners. Just last Tuesday, all the mills had closed for Fast Day. Binnie grinned, remembering how more than half of the household had awakened even earlier than usual "to enjoy the holiday."

Whack! A flying fist landed on her nose and sent tears smarting into her eyes. "Ow!" she yelped as she shoved the short, fat, dimpled arm off her face. "Brat!"

Drat that Aleck. He loved to climb from his trundle bed into the warm spot left by Mama, but he tossed and turned as if he slept alone. Turning on her side, Binnie wrapped an arm around the chubby, balled-up body and nuzzled the back of his neck. Aleck in sleep still had the extra soft, milky-moist skin of a baby.

"Move, Binnie, move!" Mama's voice, shrill in anger, came from the kitchen.

Aleck squirmed and corkscrewed around to face Binnie. "You're hoggin' the pillow. Move, Binnie."

"Of course I'm lying on the pillow. It's my pillow, dummy."

"And I told you and told you. Don't you never take any kisses 'nless I give them to you," he scolded.

"You owe me two for hitting me on the nose," Binnie answered.

Aleck put up his hand, feeling like a blind man for her face. "I'll pay now."

Eyes shut tightly, he started showering her with kisses. Wet and enthusiastic kisses cascaded down her cheeks, more kisses skidded off her nose and still more kisses bounced off her chin.

"Stop! Stop! I don't want to be killed dead by a kissing machine." A laughing Binnie rolled out of bed to escape. The more you loved Aleck, the more love he asked for and got.

Just the sight of Aleck's round, ruddy face with its upturned crescent mouth made most people smile. The women in the house chuckled, called him "little man" or "the little general," and reached into their apron pockets to find a horehound or gibraltar candy for him. He took for granted his right to their attention and climbed into their laps whenever it pleased him.

Sometimes he went too far for Binnie. When he rolled his eyes and put on a smarmy, sweet-innocent air, she rebelled. She would pinch his bottom and threaten to leave him in the boggy land by the Big Woods. Then, faster than the weathervane on First Church, he would turn to beg his way back into "my big Binnie's" favor. There was not much doubt. Alexander James Howe at the age of five had a well-developed gift for winning people.

"Bin-nn-ieee! If you don't get yourself out of bed . . . ." Mama's tone of voice plainly said this was her last call before she let her hand fall heavily on Binnie's bottom.

From being a lady of leisure she had become suddenly a lazy slug-abed. Arabinia Jane Howe sighed. If only Aleck would take charge of dressing himself. If only there were no boarders to be fed.

"C'mon. Reach," she commanded him. "Reach for the sky."

Dutifully, he stretched his arms straight up over his head as she pulled his nightshirt up and off. Pull, tug and push. From long practice, Binnie could dress Aleck in less than two minutes. She took a little longer to dress herself only because of having to braid her hair. Another minute more to ready and push the trundle under the big bed and at last Binnie could head for the kitchen.

"Mind you do a good job and don't take forever," she warned Aleck and left him to his chore of plumping the pillows and smoothing the bedclothes on the big bed.

In the kitchen, Mrs. Howe was mixing batter with short, hard, punishing strokes. She tossed her head, throwing the single loose plait of fading blond hair back over her shoulder. She had not stopped to pin it up this morning. Mama looked up and greeted Binnie.

"About time. Do the platters. I've fallen behind today, like a cow's tail."

Picking up her mother's last words, Binnie's imagination placed Mama stiff and upright at the end of a cow. She'd like to see any cow try to swish Mama's solid barrel shape. The picture was too much for Binnie's gravity. She snickered and then guffawed.

"Rude child. Save your levity for your free moments. To work, Binnie," her mother commanded, too busy even to be curious about the laugh.

The bustle of preparing breakfast for sixteen boarders had its own rhythm, a rhythm that picked up speed at the

sound of the clanging bells dismissing the workers. Five minutes' walk from factory to house: The crowd of hungry
women would be pouring in soon. Mrs. Howe sliced bread;
Binnie filled baskets with crackers; Aleck fetched and carried cups, silverware and pitchers. On this gray, sloppy day,
they would demand twice the usual amount of steaming,
strong coffee and tea.

Feet stamping, voices calling, the women hustled in,
bringing with them the rain. Drops fell in a fine spray as
they shook and hung wet cloaks on the pegs in the entry-
way. There would be mud aplenty for Mary Kate to sweep
up when she came in to work after breakfast. Binnie sniffed.
She hated the prickly, nose-stuffing smell of wet wool that
was filling the front of the house.

The women pushed into the dining room, pulling in skirts
as one squeezed past another and scraping chairs against the
bare wood floor as they sat down around the two long tables.
The first to sit began eating without waiting for the others.
With thirty minutes for breakfast and ten of those spent
walking to and from the mill, there was no time for manners
and no pause between swallows.

Edging around the tables with platters of hotcakes was a
tricky business. In the Howe family, only Binnie was both
skinny enough and quick enough. Aleck was banished to the
old backless chair in the kitchen to spoon his own hot porridge. Mrs. Howe stood in the doorway, passing pots of
freshly boiled coffee to Binnie, who passed them on to the
seated women. Voices rose around her, fighting one another
to be heard.

"A little freshet like this will never close them down. Besides, we just had a holiday last week."

"My spindle can scarcely turn, my thread is that slack I won't hardly get my stint done." Phoebe Little's complaining voice rode up over the others.

Maria Teasdale, who was Binnie's favorite among the boarders, had labeled their meals, "Gobble, Gulp and Go Time." Now catching Binnie's eye, Maria laughed, winked and amended it, "More like gabble, gabble than gobble, eh, Binnie?"

"Even if we do lose money by it, I'd welcome a day off," said Mrs. Penfield. "My feet always ache so much from standing in front of those machines all day, but in this rainy weather, my bunions are acting up besides."

"They'd better not shut down. My pockets are to let," said Dorcas Boomer. "I can't afford any more holidays."

Binnie threw a look of disgust at the last speaker. It figured that Dorcas would not have a penny saved. If she wasn't buying silks to strut in, she was ordering new lotions, laces, ribbons and bonnets. She took great pride in her looks, and enough people admired the reddish hair and pale white skin to confirm her own good opinion of herself.

To Binnie's eye, the delicately veined skin looked blue as skim milk and the popping greenish eyes reminded her of overripe gooseberries. Binnie thought her vain, foolish and a hypocrite. Dorcas talked big about being a woman of independence, but the be-all of her life was to get married. Whenever a man—old or young, deacon or overseer, any man at all—came into sight, she put on what Binnie called her "man manners."

Swishing and swaying her broad-beamed backside, Dorcas would flutter her sandy eyelashes at him and push her coarse, gravelly voice up high into a purring, simpering sing-song. To Binnie's great disgust, the man always smiled back at Dorcas. Binnie marveled at how stupid some men could be. Especially the bosses. Bosses were supposed to be more able, smarter than a plain worker. How could they not see through Dorcas's posings and acting?

"A pot of tea, Binnie girl. Surely you can find *one* pot of tea for me?"

"Is there no hash this morning, Mrs. Howe?"

Commands and more commands to be filled immediately. Binnie accepted the commands matter-of-factly. In her experience, children were born to be ordered around and escaped only by growing up. Suddenly, it occurred to her that Mama had *not* escaped. Every boarder in the house was her boss. If Alice Howe didn't cater to the women, they would go board at some other house on the corporation list of acceptable places. Then the widow Howe would become the *penniless* widow Howe with some very hungry children as a consequence. It seemed a backward kind of world where a mother had to put the desires and wishes of other people first in order to take care of her own children.

Binnie frowned and shook her head. Such a state of affairs made growing up hardly worthwhile. But she had more pressing problems to solve just now. Like how to whisk away the last of the hotcakes for her own breakfast. Already the chairs were scraping back, the plates being passed to one end and stacked. Maria Teasdale was looking at Grace Little with some concern.

"Is your tooth so troublesome still, Grace? Would you rather one of us took your looms for the remainder of the day?"

A gray-faced Grace shook her head "no," and Maria

18

turned to Binnie. "I finished *The Scottish Chiefs* last night and I won't be taking it back to the library until pay night."

Her remark carried to Binnie an unspoken but clearly understood permission to borrow the book until that time.

A tall eighteen-year-old, Maria sympathized with anyone who liked to read. It was the circulating libraries as much as the chance to earn hard cash that had drawn her to Lowell. She had joined no less than three libraries and considered the twenty-five cents a week well-spent. She never tangled herself (or Binnie) in rules about what was suitable reading for young girls: Once she read a book, she willingly shared it.

Some thought her too brainy, too aloof, but Binnie approved of both her inquiring mind and reserved manner. And everyone admired Maria's looks: the masses of waving honey-colored hair, her wide-spaced gray eyes and waist as small as a sapling tree.

Binnie's private ambition was to walk, talk and look like Maria Teasdale when she grew up. Alone and in secret, sometimes she practiced the first two, but she wasn't quite sure what to do about the third part of her desire. Time might stretch Arabinia J. Howe into a tall person, magic might lighten and curl the string-straight brown hair, but only a miracle could change the deep-set, molasses-dark eyes. Binnie held onto her firm belief that it could happen but preferred not to examine too closely the how of it.

Now, with a quick flip, Maria pulled a hood up over the waving hair. "Ho, ladies, wait for me," she called and hurried to the door.

The door slammed shut, and in the sudden silence Binnie could hear the clatter out in the kitchen. Mrs. Howe had already started boiling potatoes for the midday dinner. Moving into the kitchen, Binnie found the plate of hotcakes that she had saved for herself. She ate with a total disregard for the stacks of dirty dishes and tilting cups that crowded the table and every other flat surface in the kitchen. On school days, the morning's dirty dishes waited for Mary Kate, the Irish girl who came in to help. At least once each day, Mama thanked Divine Providence out loud for Mary Kate and Binnie added a silent amen, for otherwise the job fell to her and Aleck.

Girls who were willing to hire out were scarce. Those who traveled from all over New England to Lowell came for the good cash wages that operatives earned in the many mills, not for the piddling pay of a hired girl. Good luck and Mary Kate's two burly brothers had sent her to the Howes.

A little dumpling of a girl, Mary Kate was slow-witted. The brothers with whom she lived preferred to have her "under the wing of a good woman," as they put it, than working in the noisy and confusing mills. The arrangement suited both parties. Mary Kate, who could easily turn mattresses or carry chamber pots to the outhouse, was especially delighted to be earning money like every able-bodied woman in town.

Having finished with the hotcakes, Binnie found Aleck's porridge bowl and tipped it up to drain the last finger of sweetened milk. Binnie's appetite regularly astonished people. Although small and undersized, she ate as much as a hungry blacksmith. She had a special fondness for the heels of bread and hard, chewy crusts. Now she hunted through the dishes and platters to capture any that had been left.

"Stop pawing through those dirty dishes."

Her mother's command made Binnie jump as she gave her sticky fingers a last guilty lick.

"I've told you and told you. You should fill a plate and sit down like a decent Christian to your meals. That's why none of it sticks to you even though you eat so much."

Binnie's skinny frame was a constant irritation to Mama, who prided herself on both the quality and quantity of food that she set on her table. Mrs. Howe was convinced, too, that even a little bit of food eaten under the right conditions could make a body substantial. She always ended the familiar lecture with: "Just look at me. You know I eat like a bird, but I eat properly and just look at me."

The last was sometimes said with something of a sigh, since Mama got stouter and more short of breath each year. True, she did not eat a great amount at any one meal, but Binnie's sharp eyes had noticed another fact. As a good cook, Mama felt obliged to test and taste a dozen times or more everything that she put on the fire. And, to avoid waste, all the dabs of leftover this-and-that went on her plate whenever she sat down during the day for a cup of tea.

On this cheerless gray day of scrambling catch-up, a restless demon possessed Binnie. She blurted, "But, Mama, you know that birds eat all day long. Like you, they never stop. Maybe that's why . . . ."

She broke off, appalled. A half-moment of startled silence stretched out while Mama looked measuringly at her daughter. Then her mother surprised Binnie by breaking into a trill of laughter.

"You're absolutely right, Arabinia Howe. But you're a pert, saucy girl to say so to your mama. And I'm a fool to encourage you by laughing. Make haste or the late bell will be ringing before you get to school," Mama finished with a frown and turned briskly back to her cooking chores.

"Isn't Aleck going?" Binnie's tongue almost slipped and added "again." It seemed to her that Aleck stayed home more often than he went to school.

"Too wet. He'll get a cold on his chest, and I don't want him sickening with a spring fever."

Despite Aleck's look of well-fed good health, Mrs. Howe was always worrying about illness-to-come.

In Binnie's opinion, Aleck, with his constant absences from school, stood more in danger of becoming a booby than an invalid. Because he had been born six months after Papa died, Aleck automatically collected sympathy from all adults. Binnie could not see why or how this made him more sickly or more likely to catch cold, but instinct told her that this was not the morning to point out any more truths to Mama. She collected her cloak, pail and copybook.

"If you work on your lessons this morning, I'll hear them when I come home," she offered.

"I already started," he answered with a virtuous air. Seated by the fire with a slate on his knees, he traced out the letters: *a-l-e-x-a-n-* . . .

"Great *A*," she interrupted to correct him. "Remember, names of people and places start with great letters. Great *A* and great *H* for your name."

Binnie knew that she had put off leaving for as long as she could. Reluctantly, she stepped out, pulling the door shut behind, and made a face as the rain splashed from her hood onto her chin. She cut across the lots on a diagonal toward Merrimack Street. Without Aleck, she traveled more swiftly and could give undivided attention to her own thoughts.

It was a good day for brooding on problems such as how to be your own and only boss. Binnie had long ago decided that you needed money for that. The one question remaining was: how to get piles and piles of money.

Binnie could not remember a time when the Howes had even one penny extra. As a doctor, Papa had worried more about curing people than earning money. When he died from influenza, Mama had inherited mostly promises of payment and very little cash. The move from Boston to Lowell where she could manage a company boarding house allowed Mama to feed and shelter her family. But it did not provide abundantly or leave many coppers over to clink idly against one another. Without money, Binnie thought glumly, a body could not pick, choose or be fussy in any way.

Take her skirts, for example. She felt a spurt of irritation as she hitched up her dress with one hand. Spring or winter, she always had soaked, bedraggled hems. She must be the only girl in Lowell who had her skirt hanging below her ankles. Her dresses were always made thriftily with "room to grow." Since Binnie grew so slowly and so little, they always wore out before the proper length for a young girl could be reached. Just once, she would like to have even a tiny inch of pantalette showing. Just once, she would like to look like everybody else her age.

She stepped sideways off the path to bypass a particularly deep puddle and paused. To avoid the dangers of the Acre, Binnie usually walked first toward the Suffolk Mills before turning west and south to school. But this squaring off added a long leg to the trip. Today she weighed the risk of attack against the risk of being late for school. A tardy entrance earned the delinquent a dozen whacks across the palm with the stiff wooden ruler. Binnie shivered. She chose the direct route.

Left to right, right to left. Her head swung slowly in a wary arc. On such a wet day, nobody would be hiding in the tall brown cattails that fringed the path. Her eyes scanned the alders and stunted birches that crowded down the slope and into the low-lying wetlands. Ahead on the path, just within sight, a dark blur moved and changed its shape. The movement caught her eye. Past experience had taught Binnie some hard lessons. That blur could be an arm raised high to cast a stone. She did not hesitate.

A half-spin and she was off the path, plunging through the cattails. She scrambled up the hill and dove through an opening in the woods. Wet branches of scrubby trees slapped back, hitting her shoulders, as she zigzagged up the hill. At last she reached the top and there stopped to take some deep breaths. She looked for the natural break in the growth that marked where the land fell away in a straight drop. Then she jumped down to land with a knee-bending thump in the clearing six feet below. The path that curved under the brow of the hill was barely visible and angled finally to an abrupt end at a bald outcropping of granite.

She was home free now. This way was little used, for few people knew that the main path lay just beyond the rock ledge. Adam had shown it to her the year before. Binnie used it sparingly as a shortcut and—now that she didn't have Adam to keep the bullies at bay—as an escape route. There was no time to rest on the ledge. Slipping and sliding on the wet rock, she scuttled across in a hunched running walk. A last plunge down the sloping rock face and she stood again on the big lane.

When the figure appeared directly in front of her, she was unprepared. Surprise pushed her back up against the rock and held her still. The stocky boy with spindly legs stood several inches taller than she and looked about fourteen to her.

"You." His arm, which had been raised in a hailing gesture, came down. "You're the one with the big brother. He gone away?"

Binnie nodded in dumb silence.

"Where'd he go?"

"To Harvard College. In Cambridge. To study theology." She spoke in short, scared bursts.

Should she have admitted that Adam wasn't nearby to protect her? Too late now. Confused but curious, Binnie waited with her eyes locked on the boy's face. He had black hair and thick black eyebrows that came straight across to meet over his nose. These gave him a somber air. His nose was large—not hooked or beaked, but large in the way of a part that had grown faster than the rest of his face. Over the trembling in her stomach and the racking thumps of her heart, Binnie heard him speak again. His voice had an up-and-down lilt to it that she recognized. As she had guessed, he came from the Acre.

"Father and the Master say they'll open fifteen minutes earlier and close later, too. Father says we all need more catechism, anyway."

There was a long pause in which Binnie tried to sort out the meaning of his words. "Father" was what the Irish called their ministers. "Opening" and "closing" must mean the Irish school, which was separate and apart from the town schools.

Within the boundaries of the Acre and spilling into the Half Acre, the Irish had created a small separate kingdom. Hundreds of shanties had been built and tents pitched in a cluster around St. Patrick's, the Catholic church. Fardowners, Corkonians, Kerrymen, they traded with one another, nursed one another, and fought one another in feuds carried over from the Old Country. But whenever a taunting Yankee came in sight of their territory, they banded together like wolves to attack the outside enemy. Schoolboys threw snowballs, men used fists. Both young and old carried sticks and stones into the battles.

Adam had never been a name-caller like some, but he had been a ferocious scrapper when defending himself and Binnie. Was this why the boy had stopped her to pass on the news? If the Yankees and the Irish went to school at different times, the boys could not gang up to fight one another. The possibility of peaceful comings and goings was a liberating idea that caused her hunched shoulders to relax. In the silence, she could hear the steady splat of raindrops hitting rock and the plop as the drops bounced from rock to puddles below. She began edging sideways to find a way around the boy.

He spoke again. "You run good. A wild turkey would have to trot right fast to stay ahead of you."

Binnie accepted the comment in unblinking silence. She thought he himself must have been flying to cut her off as he had.

"What's your name?" he asked.

Binnie swallowed, cleared her throat and tried to answer firmly.

"Binnie." The single word exploded like a cork from a popgun.

"Little Skinny Binnie. Binnie suits you." He showed white, pointed teeth in a wide grin, and repeated, "Skinny Binnie." His eyes—the brilliant shade of blue in a peacock's tail—were amused.

Too much. To have this strange boy laughing at her name, her shape and her size was too much for Binnie. Anger braced her backbone and she spoke with scorching emphasis.

"It's *Arabinia. Miss Arabinia Jane Howe to you*, Mr. Muttonhead."

She did not wait to see how he took her words but streaked like lightning away from him down the path. Although she never looked back, she knew positively that he was laughing at her scared-rabbit escape. A breathless Binnie slid into place on the hard, splintery bench near the front of the room, beating the late bell by seconds. She found a consolation in the ringing bell. It proved that she had needed to run. But next time . . . next time, she promised herself, she would walk away calmly, coolly. Maybe she would even thumb her nose at him the next time.

Binnie shivered and sighed. Inside was as damp and dreary as outside. There was no heat in the schoolroom. This principal saved on wood and the town's money as if it came from his own pocket. On the first of April, he had ordered the flue closed. Despite the tardy, reluctant spring, the stove pipes had been taken down and cleaned, the stove polished to a shiny licorice black. It would not be set up again until after the first frost in the fall.

Thwack! The monitor who stood behind the teacher's desk on the raised platform brought down his birch rod with a smart crack on the corner of the desk. Voices dropped away as the pupils rose to stand with heads bowed for daily prayer.

Binnie liked the Twenty-fifth Psalm but her mind wandered today away from the words. What did the Irish do to open the day in their school? Binnie knew it was because they objected to the King James Bible readings that so many refused to send their children to public school. Somewhere she had learned, too, that they had a different Bible. But surely the pupils didn't all read that churchy-Latin? She wondered how Gospel Truth which supposedly came from God could be one thing for Protestants and another for Catholics. How could anyone tell which truth was the right truth? Was there in fact any *true* truth? That last was an unsettling idea, one that she preferred to abandon.

Last year, Binnie had had a best friend who listened to her odd thoughts. But Louiza Whipple no longer occupied the place next to Binnie. Weezy had moved West to live with a married sister who needed her help with the babies that came every year. Whenever she thought about the loss, Binnie got depressed all over. Her strong sense of fairness rescued her by reminding her of this year's other change. While there was no Weezy this year, neither was there any Mr. Hills. He had finally resigned as teacher, taking with him his leather strap and the terror of his daily beatings.

Even with this happy fact, school was simply to be endured. There was no enjoyment in daily reading lessons that were repeated endlessly. Nor was there any pleasure in the ciphering that followed. She did her slateful of sums quickly enough but doubted that she could explain satisfactorily how she got her proofs. Most of her days Binnie spent sitting low in her seat, hoping to be overlooked.

By recess time, the rain had stopped. A few of the bolder, more restless boys went out for a quick game of Prisoner, using the soaked lilac bushes as jail. Binnie joined the group playing Traveler's Trunk in the back of the room. She stayed in until the last round when she tripped on the spelling of *patchouli*. She had forgotten to put the *t* in.

The memory of that near-win warmed her for the rest of the day and gave her a springy step when she walked home. At this hour, the rain-soaked streets had a forlorn look that belied Lowell's mushrooming population. She walked quickly but carefully. Although her hem was again soaked, she jumped over the puddles in the deep ruts left by wagon wheels.

"Hey, Binnie. Yoo-hoo, Binnie Howe."

Binnie jumped. For one moment, she thought that the black-haired boy had sneaked up on her again, then she saw it was a smiling young woman who hailed her.

Noticing Binnie's blank look, the woman added. "It's Elly —Elly Tompkins. Remember me? From your own house."

Dimly Binnie recalled that the woman had been one of those in the back bedroom a while back. Some of the boarders came and went away so fast that Binnie remembered them chiefly by where they had slept.

"Tell your ma she was right: I'm back. I missed all the

girls so much, I almost died of loneliness this winter on the farm. I'm glad I followed her advice and took just a leave of absence. Tell her I'm in real luck 'cause the boss is putting me in the cloth-measuring room at Mill Number 1 and this time I mean to stick it out."

Binnie remembered now. Elly was the one who had an ear for music, and the noisy machines had pained her considerably.

"I'll be by to see her," Elly promised. "I really liked your ma's house and the girls there, but this private boarding house where I am now has a piano so I can practice my music. If I'm careful with my earnings, I figure by next year I'll be studying at a conservatory in Boston. Don't forget: Tell her hello for me."

The Seavy twins had caught up with Binnie just as the woman finished speaking and waved good-bye. Binnie turned back reluctantly to the path. She disliked walking with the moon-faced blondes who were a couple of years older than she. They always spoke in tandem, making a normal conversation impossible.

"This time next year, she likely won't have to go to Boston. We'll probably have a conservatory right here in Lowell. We already got the Institute for lectures and *it's* almost the best in the country, my pa says."

The second twin picked up on cue. "My pa figured it out. Lowell's doubled itself twice over in ten years and that means before another ten years, we'll be bigger than Boston."

"Especially since everybody in town voted last week to make us a city," the first one had spoken again.

"Maybe. Just maybe," Binnie stuck in quickly. The

Seavys always made her feel contrary. "Remember: Lots of women come but they don't all stay here all their lives."

"So long as the corporations keep adding new mills, people are bound to keep coming here. They know factory hands make good money. It stands to reason they'll come," said the twin on Binnie's right side. She spoke in a sweetly reasonable tone.

"Not only that, but the Paddies gotta come to dig the canals and build the mills. And then people need shops to sell them goods, so men gotta come to run those businesses." The two blond heads were bobbing up and down in agreement as the farther twin wound up her speech. "For every one that goes away, two more are going to come in that one's place."

The twins linked arms with an air of satisfaction. They had pronounced the last word on the subject and they headed now down Merrimack Street to their father's confectionery store. Binnie stuck out a tongue at their retreating backs. The Seavys were noticeably puffed up about their own importance and social standing. It followed that they would put on airs about where they lived as well.

Binnie forgot the twins as she thought about the new book waiting for her. Her lips curled in a half-smile of anticipation.

Ahead of her, the trees were barely laced with greening buds. When those bordering the canals blossomed out leafy and full, they created grand boulevards not unlike those of the great cities in Europe. Through the open spaces, Binnie could see three of the Merrimack's mill buildings. More than half a dozen corporations had built mills in Lowell, spreading the buildings along the riverbank and by the canals, but the Merrimack, as the first to be built in 1823, held the prime spot for waterpower. Binnie judged it to be the handsomest, too.

The red brick main building with its white cupola stood tall and imposing. Flower beds separated it from the out-buildings—the picker house, the machine shop, the store-houses—clustered in the mill yard. The whole could easily be mistaken for an institution of higher learning. In fact, Adam had written that Harvard suffered by comparison with the mills at home. He claimed that the factories were prettier in design and setting if less noble in purpose than Harvard.

Binnie wondered if she would ever see the college to judge for herself. Money. It took money to travel. All her longings and goals seemed to be rooted in this question of money. How to get large sums or—better yet—a steady sup-ply of large sums? Binnie's usual practice was to pray hard though secretly for what she wanted. But she thought it a lit-tle indelicate to ask God for money. It smacked too much of that deadly sin, greed.

When she caught sight of her own doorway, Binnie's pious thoughts scattered and she exploded.

"Sweet Jerusalem and Jehoshaphat! Why today?" she groaned.

Shawl-wrapped bundles spilled over and off a small humped trunk. They blocked the front entry. Clearly, a slaver wagon had come into town today and stopped at the Howes. Those wagons and packets traveled regularly throughout New England, tempting farm women with the chance to earn hard cash. Labor for the mills was scarce and much in demand. The opening up of the West had given men too many other opportunities, so the corporations went after the only other large supply of hands: the women. Drivers got a bonus for every woman recruited to work in the factories at Lowell, Nashua and Franklin; they only laughed when the newspapers called them "slavers."

Binnie knew she should be glad, for every new boarder meant a little more money in Mama's pockets. But it also meant more work. Binnie could not help feeling put upon. She would not get to start the new book until late tonight, if at all. As she went around to the back door, her curiosity began to stir. She wondered how many had come this time and where they had come from.

Aleck was nowhere in sight and there was nobody else in the kitchen. Binnie would have to answer her own questions. Half-heard voices told her the newcomers were still sitting in the front room. She tiptoed to the hall and leaned around the stairs to get a look. Two women sat stiffly straight on the old settee listening to Mama.

Mrs. Howe was talking in the loud cheery voice of one entertaining strangers. ". . . you had heard, I see. Lowell, of course, is the first town in America to be laid out and planned for the new factories. You may rest assured, too, that with the boarding house system, the reputation and conduct of our girls is kept beyond reproach. From the very start, the corporations have had a special care for the women operatives. . . ."

Hmm. Nothing special about these two, Binnie decided. They looked exactly like all the farm women who came in with their families for church on Sundays. Only these two had been smitten with Lowell fever, as it was called, and had come to stay. The "Lowell fever" was a catching one, Binnie had noticed. Once settled in the city, sisters brought younger sisters, younger sisters brought cousins and the cousins brought their mothers.

Never before and nowhere else had so many women collected to live and work in the company of other women as in Lowell. They filled the beds in the rows of boarding houses, they crowded the dusty streets, they flowed through the dozens of shantylike stores in the center of town and overflowed the single cramped Post Office in regular flood tides. The small number of men who came to work as bosses, mechanics or shopkeepers stood out like droplets of oil in that stream of women. The men had their own boarding houses, and always they were separate and apart from the women.

In one of her more fanciful moments, Binnie had pictured the city as a giant hive and the people who came to it as swarms of worker bees. But not honey. Money. These bees came to make cloth and money instead of wax and honey.

Honey reminded Binnie. Her insides had that familiar "gone" feeling. Retreating quietly to the kitchen, she hunted for something to fill the hollows. Under a damp, carefully draped towel, she found the bakery plum cake. That must be meant for supper. No good touching that. She found the cheese and pared slices evenly from both sides so it looked

34

untouched. Two crumbly crusts of rye-and-indian, some cider. She ate quickly, trying to fill up before Mama realized that she had come home. Feeling more anchored by the food, Binnie went almost willingly back to the front room.

"Everyone comes here to view our system, as you can see."

Mrs. Howe sounded like a schoolteacher giving her pupils a lesson. She nodded her head toward the book which lay open on the smaller woman's lap. It was Papa's old account book. Once every month, usually on Sunday, Mama pasted in it an article or a poem from the newspapers that she thought worth saving. Always she cut out the reports of important dignitaries visiting Lowell.

"The Senator, Mr. Clay. Colonel Davy Crockett. The President, Mr. Jackson."

Binnie grinned to herself. She did not need any account from a newspaper to remind her of the President's visit. She had no trouble calling up the sights and sounds of that memorable day three years ago.

The whole had been one big, glorious spectacle with drums beating, banners flying, cannon booming and miles of women workers parading past the President. All the mill women had dressed in white muslin with blue sashes—except the Hamilton Corporation women, Binnie corrected herself. They had worn black sashes out of respect for the memory of their agent who had just died. Besides that, the Russell boy had shot himself in the arm during the militia salute, two drunken Democrats had been fished out of the Pawtucket Canal and Binnie had had a silver fourpence to spend any way she pleased. Now who could forget a day like that?

"Binnie, my daughter Binnie"—Mrs. Howe's voice rose sharply, nudging into Binnie's thoughts—"will carry your belongings up to your rooms."

"Oh, never, ma'am. I c'n take care of my trunk myself."

The tall one who had spoken was dressed in crumpled, rusty black silk. Her voice sounded almost as rusty as she looked. She had the patchy, peeling skin of someone who worked outdoors but never tanned. With her sloping neck and head thrust forward, she looked like an old horse that had been out plowing in the field too long. The woman smiled and Binnie decided that she must be younger than she looked. Her cheeks were still plumped out with a full set of big white teeth.

This tall one looked agreeable enough, but it was hard to tell about the other one. The smaller woman, who wore a washed-out, no-color homespun dress, looked like a mouse and acted like one. She scurried with her head tipped down into her chest so you could not see clearly her eyes or the expression on her face.

Binnie went out to pick up the bundles and in silence she led the mousey woman upstairs to the left front bedroom, the one shared by the Little sisters and Dorcas Boomer. Mama liked to fill all the beds on the second floor before putting anyone up still another flight of stairs. Those who had to take a bed in the attic usually moved down as soon as space in a bed on the second floor became vacant.

Dropping the shawl-wrapped bundle on the double bed, Binnie smiled to herself. The newcomer would be taking the other half of Dorcas's bed. No more lying alone like a rich grand lady in a big bed for Porky-Dorky.

"Help. C'mon, Binnie. We need your help."

Aleck's shouts floated up the stairs. He was trying to help the big horsey woman with her baggage. Although she clearly was strong enough to manage the domed trunk by herself, the narrow stairs made it an awkward load. Binnie went down to help. Her hands added to Aleck's kept the "up" end of the trunk from bumping on the stairs. In the attic she waved her hand at two vacant beds. Only Maria Teasdale, who relished her privacy, chose to stay in the attic. More than half of the time she had no bedmate, and sometimes not a soul in the other beds.

"You can have either one of those," Binnie told the woman and left abruptly.

Aleck might stay to chatter but she, Binnie, could not afford to linger. She still had to carry in the evening's load of wood from the woodshed. The lamps were low on oil and the wicks had to be trimmed before supper. No need to look at the clock in the front room. The dismissal bells would warn her when the women would be coming in.

Supper for Binnie was almost a restful hour and often a pleasant one. The women, finished for the day, took their time over the evening meal; they enjoyed a second or third cup of tea and gossiped about the day's work. Binnie liked to stand in the doorway listening to their conversations.

This night, the nosey ones made the talk livelier as they poked about, asking questions of the newcomers. The two women were not related and indeed had just met on the long ride down from Vermont in the slaver's wagon.

The mouse, as Binnie called her, said only that her name was Harriet Smith. She offered nothing more and quickly put her hand back up to cover the bottom half of her face.

Binnie did not blame her. If she had a big brown mole

with a single hair growing out of it on her chin, she would cover her face, too.

The other, Florilla Nappet, said that she had come from a farm outside Pownal. With an apologetic smile, Florilla added that she and her brother's new wife had agreed about as well as cat does with dog. In the end, the bride had declared the house too small for two grown women. How her brother would manage with the planting and haying this summer, Florilla did not know. His wife was a domestic creature who fussed about the house all day long and refused absolutely to help in the fields.

"You don't suppose he's worrying about you, do you? You're better off here, beholden to nobody. Earn as much as you can, and what you earn, you can spend as you please," Dorcas said with a smug look.

"What kind of work did you think to take?" asked another.

"You must sign to work for a year, you know, and you can't leave without giving them two weeks notice." Phoebe Little's whispery voice commanded attention even in the hub-bub.

"Phoebe, why do you want to worry them with the regulations? They don't have a notion yet as to the work they may be doing," protested Mrs. Penfield, the widow from the back bedroom.

"She's tall," Grace said, eyeing Florilla. "You'd make a good dresser. Tall girls can handle the dressing frames more easily," she explained to Florilla.

"What! And have to sit in that hot, damp, closed-up dressing room? You can't deny the smell of that sizing stuff is

38

the most disagreeable smell. You're better off in the carding room. Carders quit earlier than some and the work's not so hard as some."

Harriet Smith looked confused and Florilla's head bobbed back and forth, eyeing the speakers.

"If it's money they want, they'd best take a couple of looms in the weaving room. A smart, spry girl can make up to four dollars a week." Dorcas advised.

The women broke into laughter and some hooted.

"You're worse than the corporation," Maria said bluntly to Dorcas. "Next you'll be painting roses over the gates and telling us that corporations is spelled P-a-r-a-d-i-s-e." She directed her explanation to the two new women: "Let one woman once earn as much as four dollars a week and they puff it around that *all* the women here *always* earn that much. But the truth is that you are more likely to clear about two dollars a week once you've learned the work. That's after they take out what you owe for board. They pay cash monthly—no scrip—and Merrimack's payday comes on the Saturday before the sixteenth of the month. Every room, every floor has plusses and minuses. Tell the agent what you like and take the job that suits your person."

"Oh, creation sakes, no! I wouldn't do that. I'm strong but I'm not so clever and I'm afeared they'll not hire me. I'll take anything they give me."

Florilla's accent and country way of talking amused Binnie but what the woman said made her uneasy, too. She didn't like to hear a grown up acting so meek and apologetic. It was contrary to the natural order of life as Binnie saw it.

"Stuff!" Maria said with an impatient wave of her hand.

39

"You needn't fear that you'll be idle. Come summertime, so many girls go home to visit their families or teach the summer session of school that the corporations are desperate for help. Why, they would hire an orang-outan or a chimpanzee if either applied to work."

Binnie giggled out loud. That was a mistake, for it reminded Mama that she was listening and not working. With a jerk of the head, Mrs. Howe nodded Binnie into the kitchen to start washing up the dishes.

A good landlady, Mrs. Howe herself took the two women to introduce them to the overseers and ask about jobs. Neither of the new boarders had had the kine pox, so on Friday afternoon they went again to be vaccinated at company expense by Dr. Barlow. All in all, it took a week to finish the business of settling them into jobs. And, as the days grew steadily longer, Binnie grew too occupied with her own needs and schemes to spare any thoughts for the boarders, new or old.

Spring had made a sloppy, sour beginning in April but the first days of May were like new seed pods. Each one opened brighter, fuller and with more lush promise than the last. The sun drank up the dew that lay on the grass and heated the blood under Binnie's skin. She itched and scratched where her flannel chemise lay heavy against the skin and tried to figure out a way to shed it. Since Mama ruled that chemises were worn until June 1 regardless of the weather, Binnie could only long for a magic spell to hurry the days.

Weighted by clothes, Binnie relished twice as much the freedom of bare feet pushing into sun-warmed earth. She walked very slowly to and from school and marked off the last days of school with tiny chalk lines like a sun's rays around her inkwell in the corner of her desk. In the house she darted from room to room, doing work rapidly so that she could escape back outdoors.

When Mama asked her to pick new greens for salad, she agreed gladly. South of Chapel Hill, the meadows were carpeted with dandelions. If two went to do the picking, it would take no more than an hour to fill the baskets.

"We need pick only enough for tomorrow, and afterward we can play Battle if you like, Aleck. I'll show you where there are right strong violets so you can have the best soldiers ever," Binnie said, coaxing Aleck to join her. The promise of his favorite game would make him better company during the day. Binnie stepped out briskly ahead of Aleck.

"Binnie, I bet I know more than you do. Listen, listen . . . ."

Feeling generous, Binnie slowed her pace to fit Aleck's short legs and bent her head to give him the attention he asked for.

"Who is the straightest man in the Bible?"

That was an old one. He must have heard it just today at school. Binnie kept her face sober and thoughtful as she pretended to guess.

"Do you mean the most upright? I can't imagine. All the patriarchs, I guess."

"No, no. Who, I said . . . no . . . ." Aleck was slapping his leg with glee and laughing so hard he could hardly talk. He took a deep breath to steady his voice and started again. "Who is the straightest man in the Bible? Give up? Joseph, for you know, the Pharaoh made a *ruler* of him!" And he collapsed into laughter again, his mouth wide open and pot-belly jiggling.

Like a yawn, his laughter was catching. Binnie laughed both at him and with him. In the field, they dropped to their knees and picked in a companionable silence. Aleck's small, fat fingers pulled up the dandelions, roots and all.

"Just the leaves, Aleck. Just break off the leaves. It saves work later if we don't have roots to cut off. Don't forget: only the skinniest and youngest ones," Binnie reminded him.

Neither of them liked the bitter taste of the tough leaves on the bigger plants. Just the thought of those leaves made Binnie's mouth pucker wryly. At last, Binnie decided it was time to play Battle and they moved over to the side where the meadow met the woods. Now they hunted and picked the dark blue violets which grew in abundance there.

"Get set . . . ." Binnie warned.

Each held a flower by the stem and locked the green spurs one into the other.

"Go!" Binnie shouted and they jerked the stems hard.

One violet flower flew off, one dead soldier to be laid aside. Fortunately, the dead soldier was hers. Aleck had found a good flower that laid low at least ten of Binnie's before losing its own head. A pity that the heads flew so far. Binnie wished that she could rake the scattered heads and stems into her apron.

Granny Anna Folger, the old lady who dealt in dried herbs and medicines, paid fourpence for a basket of violets. She used them to make a dark, slimy tea that cured canker sores. Mrs. Howe was one of many who preferred Granny's dried herbs, flowers and teas to almost anything the druggist sold.

"No fair, Binnie. You weren't even looking. My soldier wasn't even ready when you pulled. No fair."

Aleck was already whining. No chance of picking any extras today. Wings whistling, a great cloud of passenger pigeons darkened the sky above and reminded Binnie of the time passing. To speed Aleck up, she played bear, growling at his heels, and he trotted home faster and faster, shrieking with laughter and make-believe fear.

Both of them pulled up short at the sight of the man sitting on the stool in the kitchen. Men were in short supply in Lowell. Never before had there been one sitting at ease in their kitchen. The man's bold brown eyes inspected the children with great interest. With equal interest Binnie and Aleck inspected him back.

He was a small man, neat and compact like a bird. A dusty canvas cap covered dark curly hair, and a red bandana around the neck threw still more color into his smooth apple-red cheeks. He stood up and to Binnie's astonishment, swept them a shallow bow.

In that moment, Binnie committed herself to liking him, no matter who he was, for no man had ever before given her the courtesy of a bow.

" 'allo, chirren. Me"—at this point one finger jabbed his chest—"am .... Iyam Andre Malenfant. Frenchy, *oui*." He smiled at them and a dimple appeared and disappeared in one cheek.

"What'd he say? Binnie, what's he talk so funny for?"

"Shush. Don't talk about people to their faces," Binnie

muttered. She pulled her shoulders back and hoped she looked taller. Mama always said that a straightness of the back could make up for any lack of inches. Binnie smiled back at the man, dipped in a half-curtsy, and introduced herself and Aleck by their full names.

Mrs. Howe, who had come into the kitchen, nodded approval of Binnie's manners. "He understands better than he can talk. He's Canuck come down from the border," she explained.

It was surprising how much Frenchy managed to tell them in spite of his limited English and heavy accent. He hunched a shoulder, shivered, and they understood that it had been very cold in Canada. He thought he'd like to stay a while in Lowell to warm up.

Binnie and Aleck giggled at his account of how he had come to knock at their back door. He turned his head, sniffing vigorously to show a man who had caught a scent. Then he kissed his thumb and forefinger with a loud smack and rolled his eyes heavenward. He was saying plainly that the aroma of Mrs. Howe's stew had drawn him to their house. No wonder Mama had invited him in for a meal. This Frenchy had touched her soft spot, her pride in her cooking.

Now he made a fist and swung it in a knocking motion. He put two hands together, the fingers slanted to touch and make a steeple. He was a carpenter who could patch the roof if it needed mending.

Mama's eyes were gleaming and her cheeks creased with a big smile. She looked remarkably like Aleck when he was given a piece of candy. Most carpenters in Lowell were too busy with new building to be bothered with niggly little re-

44

pair work. Briskly, Mrs. Howe led Frenchy around the kitchen, pointing out different jobs. To pay for his supper, he fixed the latch on the back door and braced two sagging shelves in the pantry. He whistled tunefully as he went about his work.

The happy air in the kitchen was broken for Binnie when she saw Dorcas Boomer standing in the doorway. She might have known Dorcas would show up. Old Porky-Dorky could smell a pair of trousers from a mile off.

"Anything I can do . . . . Oh, you have a visitor." Her voice took on a high, syrupy tone and her hand went automatically to pat and smoothe her hair. "Is he staying?"

"Not for long and *not here*," Mrs. Howe answered, looking sharply at Dorcas. "You want something, I'll come out front shortly. People crowding the kitchen slow me down."

As Dorcas flounced out, Mama motioned Frenchy to look at a rotting window frame. Then they got down to serious talk about major improvements as well as repairs. Mrs. Howe explained—with some difficulty—that these depended on the corporation, which made all such decisions and paid the bills. She did make it plain that he could not sleep in the woodshed as he had asked.

She said, "Go where a body is alone. Help a lady." Mama made motions of swinging an ax and stacking a woodpile. Turning to Binnie, she added, "You show him the way to Granny Anna's. She ought to have room for him."

"Granny Anna's?" Binnie's deep voice almost squeaked in startled surprise. She could not imagine that stringy, sour old woman welcoming anybody. Anna Folger—called Granny Anna by everyone in town—had a temper that was more changeable than the weather. She was as likely to bop him with a broom for being foreign and talking funny as take him in to board. What had gotten into Mama? After smiling and feeding and planning out work for him, her lack of hospitality mortified Binnie.

"But why? Don't you like him, Mama?" she asked.

"Liking has nothing to do with it. The regulations say I can't, that's why. This isn't a hotel, you know." Even though the Canadian had gone outside, Mama had lowered her voice.

"But letting him stay in the woodshed isn't the same as having an outsider in the house, and it would be easier for him to do the work," Binnie protested.

"Binnie, I *know* that! But the corporation holds *me* responsible for the moral welfare of the boarders and that means we can't have that Frenchy on the premises. You don't put a fox to sleep in a hen house and I can't trust . . . . Just do as I say and do it quickly. Take him as far as the bridge and he can find his way from there. Hurry up!"

There was no mistake. Mama was exasperated now. Binnie shut her mouth and went outside to find Frenchy. He was bent over a basket which stood upright between his legs. It had one side flat, the other curved out like a bell. On the flat side the woven basket had two leather straps which he slipped one over each shoulder. Now the pack basket lay flat against his back. Binnie thought it a neat, economical way to carry one's belongings. It reminded her of the way Indians traveled.

Because she was still ashamed of Mama's rudeness, Binnie walked almost to Granny's house with him. She gave him the biggest smile she had as she pointed to the left fork in the path. He nodded, smiled back, and said, "*Au revoir.*" He took the fork up the hill, walking with the high-stepping strut of a proud cat.

Suddenly thoughtful, Binnie watched him disappear into the trees. She wondered: Was it that walk of his that made Mama decide she couldn't have him on the premises? Binnie walked slowly toward the bridge. Finally, she shook her head. She preferred to blame Porky-Dorky for Mama's snappishness. When Mama said that about not trusting, she must have had Dorcas on her mind.

In a burst of speed, Binnie rounded the bend and saw two figures at the approach to the bridge. The figures were dancing back toward her. Too late, Binnie tried to check her running steps. Like a flying wedge, she had already come between and forced them further apart. All three stood still with surprise. In that moment of frozen stillness, Binnie recognized one of them, but just barely.

It was the Irish boy with the black hair. His face was filled with fear and pain. One black eyebrow rode high in his forehead, pushed up by a gross swelling of the eye beneath. The other eyebrow had a cut at the end of it. Blood from the cut was oozing slantwise down into his ear. He was clearly in the middle of taking a beating.

As understanding hit her, Binnie cringed. Muttering jumbled, disconnected words, she put one foot back and began exploring the ground behind her for retreat.

The Irisher's feet were shuffling in the dirt, moving him in a half-circle around Binnie's left side. His fists had come up, one to guard his face, the other poised to jab out. His

eyes had the watery glaze of tears, but he was plainly determined to return some of the pain he had received.

Binnie gulped. She could not tell if he recognized her.

"Pleasegod . . . pleasegod . . . pleasegod . . . ."

That blatting croak like a wounded frog was her own
voice running together a prayer for she knew not what.
Blowing in and out of her head were the sounds of panting,
half-choked sobs and someone else's words.

"Get the . . . stick. . . . Get . . . for . . . God's sake. . . ."

The words gathered speed and force. They became a yell,
the yell a command directed at her:

"Girl . . . do you *hear*? . . . *Get that stick!*"

The voice rising in a shriek stirred Binnie's frozen
body. She backed further away and looked around. She saw
a big heavy-bottomed farm boy and a stick lying in the dirt
at his feet. Crooked and heavy, the branch from an old oak
must have just dropped from his hands. It made a deadly
club. With it, the farm boy had an almost killing advantage.

The naked violence of that club terrified Binnie, but she
was even more outraged by the unfairness of it. Even steven,
fight fair. The unwritten rules for fights tumbled through
Binnie's mind.

But what could *she* do? In any tug-of-war over the
branch, the fat farm boy would surely win. He outweighed
Binnie and the Irisher put together. Could she turn that

somehow to advantage? He had a clumsy look to him as he bent to pick up the branch.

With a sudden dart, Binnie rushed toward him and kicked hard. Once, twice. She got him in the shins and then she missed. Again Binnie's foot swung and now she aimed for the branch. She connected with it solidly, enough to send it away from them all. A last sideways dash took her out of his reach.

"Why, you piglet . . . I'll cowhide you for that." He bellowed and shook his fist at her but kept his eyes fixed on the Irish boy.

Binnie ducked down and scooped up a handful of loose moist dirt, which she packed into a ball. Then she threw it overhand as hard as she could.

"*Eee . . . yow!*"

The dirt had landed in a shower on the fat boy's face. His hands brushed and swept at his face while his mouth blew and spit to get rid of the dirt. He was still shaking his head when the Irisher leaped forward. The smaller boy peppered his enemy's head, chest, shoulders, the fists flying to land anywhere they could. The volley of flying fists lasted less than a minute. Abruptly, the other boy twisted away and ran back over the bridge. From the other side, he shouted threats and curses before backing down the road out of sight. It was a coward's retreat, Binnie thought.

Slowly the Irish boy sank down on the grassy bank, his shoulders heaving with sobs. Binnie's own legs were shaking still and she sat down quickly. The trembling came not from fear, she told herself, but from all that hard kicking.

Now that the fight was over, Binnie could hardly believe that she had dared to take part in it. A sudden breeze shocked her sweating skin into a ripple of goose pimples and she shivered with a long shudder that left her limp and relaxed.

As the boy's pain-filled, teary sobs slowly changed to the dry, racking, need-breath kind, Binnie was careful to look straight ahead. To hear a boy—a bigger one—cry was more embarrassing than to see him in his underwear. Wiping her sweating palms down the sides of her skirt, she reached up her sleeve for a handkerchief. It was a dingy, wadded-up thing but enough unused to take some of the blood, dirt and tears from his face. Silently she passed it to him, and silently he used it.

The Irisher dropped Binnie's handkerchief on the grass between them without looking at her.

"Hel-lll sweat! I hope the Deuce takes that fellow! My grandfa'r came to Boston from the Old Country before this century turned and . . . why, I was born right here. I got as much right as him to walk here or anywhere in this country, damn him! People like him make me wanna be more Irish than Saint Colmcille himself!"

Binnie could easily believe it. She knew too well that contrary feeling. Just let someone push her too hard to be a model girl: obedient, neat and dutiful . . . and she always behaved to the contrary for spite. Mama's exasperated description was: "There are good girls and then there is our Binnie."

"But, he—not him, no, nor nobody'll drive me away from where I want to be." The Irisher was working himself up into a rage again. Dark color rose in his face, giving it a dull liverish look.

To keep him tamped down, Binnie said, "He can't. You're only teasing yourself for nothing."

He looked at her and for the first time something like a smile worked across his puffy face. "You were a brick to do that." There was a pause and he added, "Skinny Binnie." And now he did smile, a full smile that showed his white teeth.

She nodded and said nothing about the "skinny Binnie." He wasn't really interested in what she had to say, anyway. The rage had boiled up enough to make him sit very straight.

"Why, when I get my money, I'll make that fat clod and all the common ruck like him be sorry."

"Do you have money?" Binnie asked, a little confused by the new direction of his remarks. She had never heard of a Paddy with money.

"No, but I'm going to get rich. I'm going to get so rich that when I go sweeping into the Stone House Hotel, Mr. Upton will bow down and say 'Yes, master. What can I do for you?' And he'll lick my boots clean, if I tell him to."

"How are you going to get rich?" Now it was Binnie who sat up straight. She was alert and curious. His longings were amazingly like hers. Had he solved the problem that had been plaguing her so this past year?

"I haven't exactly settled yet. I'm going to work, of course."

"In the mills?"

"Naw. My ma won't let me. First I have to do the high school, she says. Then, she'd like for me to be a priest. But I'm going to work and I'm going to make so much money and be such a big boss that all the sow-faced, suet-brained chowderheads in the whole of America will beg for a chance to work for me."

It was just a dream; he didn't really have a plan. Although Binnie was somewhat disappointed, the boy seemed restored to good spirits by his talk. Reluctantly, Binnie stood up. It was time and past time to go home. As they walked across the bridge, Binnie decided to tell him how well she understood what he felt. She did it indirectly.

"I always wanted a piano for our front room."

"Do you like music so much, then?" He turned to look at her. The black eyebrows rode up higher than ever to give him a look of disbelieving surprise.

There was a long pause. Binnie squirmed inside, for she had not planned to say anything else. In a way that she didn't fully understand, the fight they had shared tied them together. Certainly what she had done put him under obligation to her. Yet here she was feeling as if she owed him a confidence in return.

"No." She plunged into an explanation. "It's that Mama always wanted one. What I mean to have when I grow up is a house, a whole house that belongs just to my family. A big white house with lots of big rooms . . . and there'll be no sharing of beds or bedrooms, no boarders. Just me and my family."

There. She had blurted it all out. The dream was told for the first—and she hoped the only—time to another human being. In her mind's eye, Binnie could see the rooms down to the last piece of furniture and the steel engravings that hung on the walls. Some pieces were old, like the beloved mahogany secretary from Papa's family; some were new, like a piano in the corner. Mama would sit in a cherry rocker and embroider while Binnie read aloud to her under the light of an astral lamp. Binnie always wore a pink dress with rust piping in that scene. But the best part was that nobody else came in and out of the room.

"Boott's," he said, nodding thoughtfully.

Binnie was startled. How could he have known that she had modeled her dream on the house of the Merrimack agent? She always slowed her steps and stared at the white Greek-columned house. Once, at dusk, she had crept through the front garden to peek in the window at an elegant wallpapered room.

"You need a lotta money."

True. She was aiming high. Kirk Boott was a haughty man, who stood at the top of the social heap in Lowell. He had laid out the whole community of factories to start with and now supervised all the Merrimack mills for the absent owners. Nothing but the best was good enough for "His Imperial Majesty," as people called him.

"You need a heap of money," the boy repeated.

Binnie thought of her little silver hoard tied in a handkerchief and hidden behind the mantel clock at home. She nodded sadly in agreement.

"What you need is to become a boss. Bosses are always well-to-do. They make twice and more than anybody else in the factory."

True enough. But Binnie had never seen or heard of a lady—no matter how nimble, clever and experienced—who got to be a boss. "Don't all the overseers and such have to be men?" she asked.

"Well, anyway you could *start* making money by doffing. Lots of girls your age are doffers and I bet you're faster than most of them."

"My mama says those mills are dirty places and bad for

the health of a growing girl. That it goes against the natural order of things for people to be cooped up so long every day." Binnie's shrug said she did not agree with such overly nice notions of cleanliness and order.

"I been looking every week in the Lowell *Advertiser*. Rand, the sash and blind place, wants a smart young fellow for apprentice. But it says seventeen years of age at the least and none other need apply. I'm just fourteen, so-o . . . ."

It was somehow consoling to know he had looked in the paper just as she had and failed to find a way to earn money. Binnie said, "The real trouble to my getting any steady work is that I have a little brother, Aleck, and I have to watch him." Actually, Binnie thought this fact weighed against her working in the mill more than any other as far as her mother was concerned.

"Have some mites?" he asked. He had pulled a tissue envelope from his pocket and held it ready to shake some of the treat into her hand.

Binnie took a handful of the sugared caraway seeds and popped them into her mouth. As her teeth snapped the sweet, hard little seeds in two, she decided that he was a generous fellow. He was the kind of person it was easy to like and she gave him a warm look of approval.

On the corner where he had to turn off for the Acre, he paused. "Anybody ever come up to give you trouble,"—here he nodded over his shoulder toward the shanty town—"tell them you're a good friend of mine."

"Wait! Well, yes, but I don't *know* your name."

He looked surprised and then sheepish. "McCabe. Patrick. But you'd best say 'Packy' because that's how I'm

54

known. Or say the widow McCabe's boy. I'm the only one, so everybody knows the name."

Binnie waved good-by as he set off toward the Acre. Despite their depressing discussion about money, she felt very cheerful. If claiming friendship with Packy McCabe spared her from attacks by Irish bullies, she would be lucky indeed. What a pleasure it would be if she could walk straight down the street instead of slinking the long way around the Acre.

The spring session of school ended without a chance to test the value or strength of this Packy's name. Nor did she have a chance to hunt him up and talk again. The hot sunny days of May, which were so ideal for lazing and reading, moved Mrs. Howe into a frenzy of cleaning. Each day, she found one more thing to dunk in soapy water, one more carpet piece or braided rug to shake and beat, one more brass to polish. Binnie and even Aleck were sucked into the whirlpool of her efforts.

When Aleck complained, Mama said, "Idle hands are willing tools of the Devil's own work," and added yet another chore to an already full day's work. The extra jobs had to be fitted in between and around the regular chores.

Aleck sat on the kitchen floor with legs stretched out straight. He was rubbing an andiron from the front room to a high shine with good New England rum. The rich, heady smell of rum was tainted by the unpleasant smell of spirits of turpentine that Mama was using to chase ticks from the mattresses and roaches from the pantry.

While Mary Kate took down the muslin curtains for washing, Binnie raced to the store for more potato starch. To reach and stir the boiling starch, she stood on a cricket. She pushed the curtains down into the kettle with an old broomstick. The air was thick and heavy with steam, strange smells and nervous tension.

When Phoebe Little stepped into the kitchen, she wrinkled her nose over the smells. She asked, "As long as you have some starch boiled up, Mrs. Howe, would you mind just taking a couple of collar and cuff sets into the kettle? Oh, and I have some aprons from last wash that need a little stiffening, too. If you don't mind, please." Her last words were tacked on as if she had just remembered that she was a lady of good manners.

"Yes. Positively." Mama's voice rose steadily, becoming louder with each syllable. She was like the kettle, heated up to the boiling point but spilling over. "Yes. I *do* mind. No, you cannot put anything—not one thing—into that kettle. You want a load starched, you wait until I've finished my spring cleaning. And then you do it yourself. Do you hear?"

Binnie didn't see how Phoebe could help but hear, for Mama was actually shouting by the end. Phoebe was clearly taken by surprise. Her smile faded, her ever fluttering hands stopped in midair as she stared at Mrs. Howe. Binnie, too, was astonished. Mama had broken her own First Rule of being a landlady. The First Rule said you always obliged the paying boarder. Always. No matter what.

"Well-ll. I *do beg your pardon*, Mrs. Howe. Of course, I'll do them myself. DO send one of the children to tell me *when* I might be permitted to put a foot in the kitchen. With your permission, of course." The words were respectful, but her whispery voice made them mocking. Head high, Phoebe exited with the air of a queen who had been offended and would not soon forget it.

56

Mama sat down abruptly on the stool. "I refuse. I refuse to be that woman's personal laundress. Her board money don't cover that. By no means. No way."

Mrs. Howe breathed with a kind of wheeze that came from deep within her chest. Her eyes had a suspicious shine to them. Was the shine from unshed tears of rage or the watery glaze of a cold coming on? Binnie could not decide. Either way, she felt an unexpected pang of sympathy for her mother.

"Do you feel good, Mama?" Binnie asked cautiously.

Before Mrs. Howe could answer, Mary Kate spoke with smiling enthusiasm. "You sure look good, Mrs. Alice. Better than yourself."

Binnie disagreed. Neither the pink flush in Alice Howe's cheeks nor the bright glitter in her eyes that made her look younger and almost pretty was natural or right.

By the next day, Mrs. Howe's voice had taken on a hollow barking sound that made Binnie jump whenever she heard it. And she heard it often, for Mrs. Howe refused to admit there was anything wrong. She dragged herself and Binnie and Mary Kate from floor to floor putting the house back to rights. She would not stop even for one cup of tea. That worried Binnie considerably, even more than the barking voice.

At supper time, Mrs. Howe did not bother to put any food on a plate for herself. In between the chores of serving and clearing, she sat on the stool and stared blankly at the wall. For a woman whose favorite word was *quickly*, Mrs. Howe sat alarmingly still. It looked to Binnie as if Mama was losing her battle against the worsening cold and a rising temperature.

There was no warning when she gave up. Like an empty sack placed on the stool, she simply and silently crumpled: head sagged onto her chest, chest folded to her stomach and all of Mama slid off the stool in a faint.

"*Mon dieu!*" The exclamation came from Frenchy, who had just entered the kitchen from the backyard with his empty supper plate. Both he and Binnie started at the same time for the mound on the floor. Even before they reached her, Mrs. Howe had humped herself up almost on her knees. She was weakly pushing her palms against the floor to get up. Together, Frenchy and Binnie helped her to rise and steady herself. He was clucking and rattling in a stream of French. Binnie was too scared to say a word. Frenchy signaled with his eyebrows to put her in the oak rocker rather than back on the stool.

"*Le docteur,*" he said to Mama, settling her in the chair. "*Oui, madame,* she need *Monsieur le docteur.*"

"No, no doctor." Mama's hands fended them off like shooing flies. "It's only ... only a dizzy .... A cup of tea, Binnie. Pour me a cup of tea with a little honey and a drop of vinegar, and I'll be all right."

"P'raps, *madame* 'ave cure stuff? Good stuff like ze cognac? To 'elp 'er sleep."

Mrs. Howe nodded once, closed her eyes and put her head back against the chair. For one heart-stopping moment, Binnie thought she had fainted again. She was relieved when her mother's voice barked at her to hurry with the tea. She told Binnie to fetch down the brandy bottle from the top cupboard shelf. Binnie splashed it recklessly into the cup and at the sound Mama opened her eyes.

"Not too much, girl. You'll make me whiskey frisky."

Although she did not actually get frisky, the tea made Mrs. Howe talkative. Yes, she would go to bed and rest. Just until the fever broke. She gave them a steady stream of directions. For the while, Mary Kate was to come early and leave late. That way, she and Binnie should be able to keep even with the chores. Make boiled stew for dinner tomorrow. Binnie must write a note explaining it all to Mary Kate's brothers. They worried if she did not come home at the same time each night. Don't try to wash the linens until the end of the week.

Aleck sat whimpering and scared on the floor, leaning against Mama's legs. He broke into howls when Mama said he could not sleep in the bedroom with her. He refused at the top of his lungs to go up to the empty bed in the attic with Binnie.

"All right, Aleck." Mama patted his head but did not bend to kiss him. With her other hand, she poured more brandy into the tea cup and beckoned for more tea. The color had come back in a great rush to her face. She looked like an overripe tomato, red-skinned and bursting. "Make him a pallet, Binnie, in the pantry. That way he'll be close enough to me but not too close to catch anything."

In a jerky rush of movement, she stood up and headed for the bedroom, reminding her daughter that the supper dishes had to be washed. Binnie turned with relief to the familiar task and Mrs. Howe got herself ready for bed. The last thing Binnie did was to fill the pitcher with water and place it next to her mother in the bed.

"Binnie, g' night." Then with a sudden urgency, she called, "Binnie, I want you."

"Yes, Mama, I'm here."

"If anything, if you need ... Cornelia's letter ... the address is in the secretary. Or ask for Elias Howe ... over to the machine shop. He's come from Spencer to work .... "

Her voice trailed off as she slipped back into a doze. Binnie waited, tense and still. Sure enough, Mama roused herself again.

"Too young," she said to Binnie's puzzlement. "But he's kin of a kind and he knows where Cornelia ... where to find .... " She muttered something and sank back into sleep. This time it was a deeper sleep with heavy snores rattling through her open mouth.

Binnie turned away, feeling very much alone. Aleck had long since climbed into the pallet and pulled the covers over his head. The whole house was still and quiet as she slowly went up the stairs. For almost the first time in her life, Binnie wondered if she had eaten too much. She felt a little sick.

The thought brought back the picture of Mama crumpled up on the floor and Binnie's stomach gave another lurch. She pushed the picture out of her head and tried to fix on something else. It should be a treat to sleep in the attic with Maria Teasdale and Florilla Nappet. Florilla was jokey and good-natured; Maria often read until late in the night so she would not mind if Binnie did likewise.

But why had Mama been talking about that far-off Cornelia? She would look tomorrow afternoon for the letter with the address, Binnie decided.

Binnie could not remember when she had last been so tired. She was tired, too, of fighting off the sounds that were nagging for her attention. Reluctantly, she decided that it would be easier to open her eyes. All the shadows and shapes that she saw were strange unknowns; only the voice sounded familiar as it grew louder. It came to her finally that she was in the attic listening to Maria.

"Binnie, I've not had any sleep since blowing out my candle. His crying is getting louder by the minute. He'll awaken all the women in the house soon. It'll take hours to calm the house down if you don't do something about his crying now."

In the flickering candlelight, Maria's gray eyes looked frosted with ice, her lips pulled tight. Dimly, Binnie was aware of a distant crying, rising and falling. Why was she, Binnie, supposed to do something about that, she wondered. Why didn't Mama hear it? Then she remembered and groaned.

Binnie pulled herself out of bed, and staggered a second when her feet found the floor. Taking the candle that Maria was holding out to her, she felt a twinge of resentment as sharp and painful as a toothache that a grown-up Maria was expecting her, a young girl, to perform Mama's tasks. In all fairness, though, there was no reason for Maria Teasdale to feel responsible for calming Aleck. He was a Howe. Binnie was a Howe and the only one now in the house who was fit to help him.

Moving slowly down the stairs, she thought what a mistake it had been to sit up so late reading. Especially when you had to wake up in the middle of the night and take care of something. Closer to, Aleck's wails had a strangled sound to them. Half of her worried about him and half of her continued to feel sorry for herself.

"Coming .... I'm coming, you pesky boy," she called in a loud whisper.

She didn't dare call any louder for fear of waking others. When she reached Aleck, she realized that he was still asleep. The tears rolling down his fat cheeks came from tightly shut eyes. Somehow he had poked through the old sheet and the torn hem had wound itself in a thick tie around his neck. The strip ended as a sling binding one arm. Binnie gave a nervous giggle. The light woke him and his cry of "Binnie" was both grateful and a reproach at the same time.

"Have you had nightmare?" she asked.

"Big spiders, black crawly spiders bigger than a house. They waved their legs and I could see the long, long hairs on their legs. An' then they threw a web over me and I was stuck, sticky stuck . . . 'n a leg came around choking me. . . ." He shuddered and his lower lip trembled, ready to drop open in new sobs.

"No wonder," she said, putting sympathy in her voice as she began separating him from the sheet. Easy to see where that dream came from. She pulled his arm out, ducked his head through another loop of the hem and at last had him free. "Upstairs is better. Nothing, nobody can get you there," she soothed. "Besides, if any old spiders come, Florilla can knock them right down."

The last had made him laugh, but not enough. "Carry me," he whimpered and wrapped his arms around her waist.

"Oh, Aleck, you're too heavy." She sighed. He was not going to let go. "Let's try piggy back, then."

"You know what, Binnie? If the spiders was real, I bet you could scare them away yourself. You can do anything."

"Sh-sh." She warned him to be quiet.

The comfort of being plastered against her back, relieved from terror, had set him to babbling. "I bet you can run faster than Adam. You're so big and strong. When I grow up like you, I want you to be my best-ever friend and live in my house. Next to Mama, I love you best. You know that?"

She? Big and and strong? Grown-up already and able to do anything? Binnie was so startled by Aleck's words that she stopped suddenly, causing him to slide down. It had not crossed her mind before that someone could look up to her and admire her. She felt a little swelling of pride at the thought.

But if she had any puffed-up notions stemming from Aleck's words, they were quickly squashed in the days that followed. All feeling of being capable and strong oozed away under the effort of keeping up with the work. For the first time, she realized how much Mama did in the course of a day.

Mary Kate helped but did only what she was told. And if Binnie told her in words different from those Mama used, it confused her so the job didn't get done. A sulky Aleck did half of what she asked and ran outside to play every time she turned her back. She had no time to cosset and coax him back. It was easier and quicker to do the work herself. Her thumb hurt from pushing the paring knife harder to move it faster and her legs ached from racing between the kitchen and dining room. Still, supper was late, the crumbs from the morning lay unswept on the floor and the women grumbled because the coffee was cold.

Binnie was too proud to explain or beg their understanding. To those who thought to ask for Mrs. Howe, she answered, "Mama's catching a quick nap just now. She's fighting off a summer cold. She'll be up soon."

She worried, too, because her mother refused to send for Dr. Barlow. Mama insisted that Granny Folger's sweet fern tea was better medicine for ague than anything he had in his bag. Besides, the doctor cost money. Binnie's prayers at night were a tired jumble of wishing for more help of some kind and more money. She slept lightly, her tired legs twitching.

On the third night when Mama called, Binnie was instantly awake and down the stairs. The bedroom smelled of sweat, damp and sickness. To see her mother lying helpless and hot with fever pained and frightened Binnie. Mama's head lifted weakly and she motioned Binnie to change the cloth on her forehead. As Binnie got fresh cool water in the basin and wrung out a fresh cloth, Mama lurched upright and gripped Binnie's wrist.

"If anything happens to me, promise you won't let them separate you. Promise me you'll watch Aleck. If I die."

Her iron grip hurt Binnie, but Mrs. Howe's words were more painful still. Like a hard slap to the face, they left Binnie numb and breathless.

"Promise me."

Don't worry, Mama." Binnie had found her breath but could manage only a whisper. "All us A. Howes come out all right. You'll be all right and so will Aleck and me."

Mama frowned. "What are you talking about? What ... who's ... the Ahows?

Silently, Binnie willed Mama to understand. She didn't want to say it any plainer. Putting it into words out loud might destroy their safeguard. Papa, the twin boys, the girl who had come between her and Aleck—all the ones who died had different initials to start their names: Joseph Henry Howe, Rob and Richard, Martha. The ones who lived—Alice Howe, Adam, Arabinia and Alexander—were all A. Howes. She had discovered this fact when she was learning to read. It had supported her when Aleck had broken his arm, when Adam had first gone away, whenever any of them took sick. Tonight—at this moment—her belief seemed more flimsy and fragile than a cheesecloth.

Mama leaned back on her pillow and welcomed the cool comfort of the cloth on her forehead with a raspy sigh.

"Go to bed, Binnie. Quickly. It must be late. Quickly."

That last word brought a spurt of hot tears to Binnie's eyes. She turned away and went to the pallet in the pantry. Somehow on this night she preferred to sleep close at hand. She lay on her back, eyes wide, staring into dark nothingness.

When any of the boarders got sick, they went home to recover. Or to—her mind halted stubbornly for a moment—or to die. Each went back to the farm, the village, the town and the family from which she had come. Back to where they had their tap roots. But for the A. Howes, this was home.

They had no place else to go and no one else to share with them the burden of illness. No amount of money or any kind of riches could change that fact.

Binnie emptied her mind of all thoughts. Choosing her words carefully, she started to pray. She was too frightened even to bargain with God. She simply asked over and over for Mama's return to good health and strength for herself to carry out whatever fell to her lot. A merciful God might grant both.

Binnie sat up with a start. Seemingly she had lain awake the whole night, staring into the dark nothingness. Yet the sharp rat-tat on the back door said that Frenchy was here, ready to work. The thumps overhead declared positively that the women were getting out of bed, and the thin, pearly light in the pantry proved that another day had already begun. She must have slept, and heavily at that.

A dazed Binnie pulled her stiff body up and went slowly to the doorway of the bedroom. Her throat was tight and dry as she checked her mother. Mrs. Howe was sleeping restlessly, turning over and then back again. But it *was* sleep and Binnie thought hopefully that it must be a healing one.

Binnie became a blur of movement as she tried to do everything at once: dress herself, let Frenchy in, start the coffee water boiling, call Aleck downstairs to set the table. Once again and already she was falling behind in the work to be done. If she had six arms and ten legs, it still wouldn't be enough, she decided gloomily.

Her biggest worry today was what to with the fish. Twice a week, the farmer left salmon on the doorstep with the basket of eggs and the jugs of milk. Since Mrs. Howe did not have patience with any people messing in her kitchen, Binnie's cooking experience was limited to peeling, chopping and boiling everything in one pot. Florilla Nappet, coming into the kitchen, clucked sympathetically.

"You been doing so much and you just the size of a new pea. Listen, leave the dishes tonight. Let me help. I can do them when I come in. How's your ma?"

"She's right sick still, but no worse, thank you. It's this fish. Can I boil it ... for like a stew?" Binnie looked dubiously at the fish and then at Florilla.

"Well, I always roasted fish in hot coals myself. Not that we saw that much fresh in Pownal. Binnie, tell the truth, I can turn my hand to almost anything, but I don't really know a whole lot about cooking. Won't it fall apart and the bones be in everything?" Florilla looked equally doubtful.

"Me. *Je suis chef*. I know cooking," said Frenchy, wiping coffee from his mouth with the back of his hand. "In nort' in beeg woods, mens chop-chop trees. I cook for all ze mens."

As usual when Frenchy spoke, his hands and body all took part in the conversation. He thumped his chest proudly, he spread his arms in a huge circle to show how big the cooking pot was and his dimple flashed in and out.

"I fix ze *saumon*, eh, *oui*?"

Binnie's mouth hung open in surprise, making her look very like the fish that was worrying her. Could she be so lucky? Did he really know what he was talking about?

"Give me . . . 'ow you call it? Floo-er? Flower? I make a sauce."

Flour. He wanted flour for a sauce. He sounded like a man who knew what he was doing and Binnie moved happily to obey. The smell that floated through the house at dinner time was even more convincing.

Mama came awake and thought she would try a bite. She looked with increasing interest at the bits of fish swimming in a creamy sauce flecked with green sprigs, tasted a spoonful and exclaimed, "That's never dried dill in there. Who would have thought to . . .? "

Frenchy, who had sniffed and tasted through every crock and jar in the pantry to find the seasonings that he wanted, heard her and looked smug.

When Binnie poured a little of the sauce on a boiled potato, Mrs. Howe ate some of that, too, though chewing so much seemed to tire her. The boarders ate in their usual starving-locusts fashion, asked for seconds and mopped with bread at the sauce until the plates were bone dry. Binnie stirred the pot jealously to be sure there was some left for her and piled her plate with every last scrap and drop.

After eating, Binnie felt good, too good to bawl out Mary Kate who had left potato peelings in a heap on the table. She kept an ear cocked as she worked through the afternoon but Mrs. Howe slept soundly, never once making those awful rattling sounds that had alarmed Binnie.

For the first time in days, Binnie faced the evening's rush calmly and a little proudly. Everything was ready on time. Florilla came into the kitchen that night and Binnie's spirits rose still higher.

"Came to give you a hand with the washing up," Florilla said, her strong white teeth gleaming in a big smile. Her sleeves were rolled up to work and her plump, well-muscled arms looked strong and able. Since she no longer worked outdoors, her skin had lost its patchy, peeling condition. Her now-smooth complexion was the color of rich cream. She still looked like a horse, but a well-fed and sheltered one.

When Frenchy, who had been measuring the pantry wall with his string, came into the kitchen, Florilla exclaimed, "Good!" She rubbed her stomach vigorously and repeated, "Good, good."

Florilla's style of conversation made Binnie giggle. She had raised her voice to a near shout, as if by being loud she could make the meaning of her words plain to the Canadian.

Binnie, visited by a sudden inspiration, made her face solemn and asked Frenchy, "Do you make pies? You *are* a good cook. We need pies for the Sabbath. Can you help again?" He was so visibly pleased that Binnie knew she had done the right thing.

The widow Penfield, looking into the kitchen, found preparations for the Sabbath Day well under way. Frenchy was whistling tunefully as he rolled out pie dough with swift expert hands. Florilla was making short work of heating water for the weekly baths, lifting the heavy kettles easily. On a clean apron thrown over her lap, Binnie had spread out the dried beans for the bean pot. She was picking through them, cleaning out the dirt and stones.

"I take it Mrs. Howe is better?" asked Mrs. Penfield. She tugged the shawl back up on her sloping shoulders. "How can a body help, Binnie, when you never let on to us that your mother was so sick?" she scolded. "I'm going out to the Post now and I'll stop for some Cherry Pectoral at the apothecary. That's the only thing for loosening up the chest," she added and turned to leave, almost colliding with Phoebe Little who had appeared in the doorway.

Phoebe's lips were pulled together in that familiar thin line and she clutched a jar tightly against her spare bosom. One look at her and Binnie's thoughts careened wildly in silent protest. I can't wait on that selfish pig and do the house-work, too. I won't. I have enough . . . more than enough.

Phoebe, who had entered the kitchen, called after Mrs. Penfield's retreating back, "That may be so for you. But I *know* nothing works like a good plaster." She addressed the room at large then. "And, of course, a knowing hand to put it on. I shall need onion and mustard. I've brought my own goose fat. Pure goose fat. But I shall need onion and mus-tard," she repeated and waited expectantly.

Wouldn't you know it, thought Binnie wryly, as she moved to get the supplies. Even when Phoebe came to nurse someone, she acted like royalty who expected to be served. Binnie knew she ought to be grateful for Phoebe's "knowing hand." A mustard plaster was nothing that she knew how to manage. Still, Binnie found it hard to give Phoebe credit for a good deed.

"We're all to be tenants of the tomb in the end. Of course, some of us are brought sooner to the borders of the grave. . . ." Phoebe's voice sounded almost loud and quite cheerful as she went in to Mrs. Howe.

It must be she likes seeing Mama flat and helpless, Binnie decided. When Dorcas Boomer, too, turned up offering to help, Binnie wondered if she was being unfair. Especially since Porky-Dorky simply took the broom and disappeared to sweep the front room. You could hardly say she was show-ing off, because there was no man out there to see her acting the "good housewife."

The next morning while walking to church, Binnie thought again about her judgments. She walked alone. Aleck, who had been a shadow glued to her heels these past days, had insisted on staying home. In case, he pointed out virtuously, Mama needed a drink of water. Had she misjudged the women, Binnie wondered? Always Binnie had seen the boarders as "they," separate and as far from "us," the family, as the two poles of a compass are. Surely the interests and concerns of the two could not and did not meet?

Certainly they didn't share the same feelings about St. Anne's Episcopal Church where Binnie was heading. Most of the women bitterly resented its existence. Kirk Boott, who had it built and named for his wife, insisted that all his workers contribute to its upkeep. The women who belonged to every other kind of church—Methodist, Unitarian, Congregational—grumbled, and rightly so. Why should confirmed members in good standing of one Christian church be obliged to support another? It had galled them to pay out the thirty-odd cents monthly, like a tax to a foreign king, but none had dared to refuse.

Binnie was glad it had been built no matter how it had been done. She greatly admired the gray stone building with its big tower and pointed windows. Every time she entered, she thought of an English castle, and often she daydreamed a romantic story throughout the service. Today she was occupied with working out the meaning of yesterday's help.

On the one hand, you wouldn't expect to be friends with people who gave you orders three times a day or more. On the other hand, Dorcas always showed off her new bonnets first to Mama, and Grace read her nephew's letters aloud to Mrs. Howe. Once Mama was persuaded to sit down or stand still she made a sympathetic and interested audience. So was this or was this not how friends behaved with one another?

The more Binnie thought, the more she felt that "them" and "us" was too simple a way of defining life in the boarding house. She decided that some of the boarders considered her mother a friend as well as a landlady; they honestly cared about what happened to Mrs. Howe. It was possible to admit that much without feeling herself obliged to like every one of the boarders. A number of them, as Heaven must know, were decidedly unlikeable.

Binnie angled her neck to see her neighbor's hymn book better. With all that thinking, she had lost her place. She sang at the top of her lungs and her final "Amen" was filled with gratitude for having squeaked by the Gates of Hell in the week past. As the service ended, she rapidly made another decision. She had earned time off. If she skipped Sunday School, she could add hours of freedom to this beautiful sunny Sabbath. She would give herself that present.

Binnie left the church feeling newly dipped in virtue. The streets were filled with women walking arm in arm, moving slowly to and from churches and meeting houses. For the services, they had all modestly covered their heads. But it amused Binnie to note how vanity triumphed over modesty. The bonnets and calashes were made of shimmering silk and lavishly trimmed with big satin bows and curling plumes. The women kept their voices low as was proper on a Sunday.

Su-sur-rus. That was the word for the sound she heard so plainly in this Sunday crowd. Had she made up the word and then found it was a real one? Or had Adam, who knew his Latin so well, told it to her? *Susurrus,* a soft murmuring sound. It didn't just describe what she heard; it even sounded like the rustling that came from the hundreds of silk skirts. On Sundays, these were more common in Lowell than turnips.

Binnie's own best dress was of cotton calico, the small-figured print of indigo blue which the Merrimack Corporation had made famous. She ducked and dodged through the crowd, anxious to get home quickly and shuck both the Sunday dress and her too-tight shoes.

At the house, Mama came out of her doze to say that Maria Teasdale was looking for Binnie.

"Best go now before you get caught up in some book or other and forget. She's upstairs and most anxious to see you. She came twice looking for you."

Hang and dang it. There went some of her free time. Binnie was both surprised and puzzled. Of all the boarders, Maria made the fewest demands. Besides, she was always so calm and aloof, it was hard to picture her anxious about anything.

"Did she say what she wanted?" Binnie asked. If Maria had spoken for something in particular, Binnie could take it up with her now and save herself a second trip.

"No. You'll find out soon enough if you go up. Are you going or aren't you?"

Binnie left her mother fretting and went to find out.

7

If Maria had been anxious before, there was no sign of it now. As Binnie's head cleared the top of the stairs, she was greeted by a face-filling smile. Binnie wished for the hundredth time that she could look like Maria. Even in a coarse stuff gown and her work apron, Maria looked beautiful. Binnie sighed. So far as she could see, they had only two things in common: Both of them were skinny and both of them loved to read.

Catching Binnie's look, Maria looked down at her everyday clothes and shook her head. She said, "Yes. I did think to go to church this morning but then I felt indisposed. Nothing serious. Just the female complaint."

Binnie suspected strongly that it was an excuse. More than once, Maria had stayed home on a Sunday to read a book.

"In any case, I had to ready this for you." Maria's hands came out from behind her slender back and she handed Binnie a package wrapped in tissue.

"Did you want me to deliver it somewhere?" asked Binnie, a little puzzled as to what she had been called to do.

Now Maria laughed outright. "I can't have got it wrong. Today *is* the twenty-ninth of May."

"Well, yes . . . but . . . ."

"Well, then the package is yours. A gift to celebrate your Birth Day."

74

"Mine? My present?"

The surprise was doubly strong. First, that she could have forgotten her own birthday and second, that anyone should think to give her a present.

"Open it," Maria urged. "Back home my papa and brothers always made a holiday of my Birth Day and I thought . . . . You do your best to attend to us. And so . . . ." Here Maria shrugged. "Open it, unless you're afraid it will bite you."

Binnie bent her dark head over the package and untied the string very slowly. Her eyes glistened and she caught her breath as the paper fell away. Two books. No, one titled book bound in soft red morocco leather. The other a journal or notebook with blank pages and stiff covers of straw pasteboard. And with that, a sharp steel pen to write in it.

Binnie sniffed hard and kept her head down. She didn't dare look up at Maria, who always got embarrassed when people showed too much feeling. Binnie sniffed again.

"I . . . I like so much the smell of new leather," she said and thought that she had covered up well. Her voice wobbled, but only a little. "I have a library now. Thanks to you and Adam. He gave me *Aesop's Fables*. He didn't need it because at Harvard he would be reading the original Greek. He made me a present of it."

Before she finished, her voice had risen until she was almost singing with happiness. She bent again to read the title of her new book.

" 'Tis one of William Wirt's. You enjoyed reading his book, *Letters of the British Spy*, remember? I thought to get you something of Jane Austen's, but this seemed more fitting for your day."

Gold letters gleamed softly from the spined book. Patrick

Henry. The name sounded faintly familiar to Binnie. Where had she heard it before? What was so special about his life and why was it so fitting for her day?

"Patick Henry was a leader in the South during the Revolution and an orator who moved the people by his speeches and passion for liberty," Maria told Binnie. And then, with the relish of one who is delivering a thunderbolt, she added, "You and he share the same Birth Day for he was born on *May 29, 1736, just one hundred years ago today.*"

"Truly, Maria? Honestly and truly, Maria? I do thank you. I do."

Binnie could not contain her delight any longer. She was dancing now, impatient and eager to share her excitement somehow, somewhere, with someone. She gave a little crow of happiness and dashed down the stairs, shouting all the way.

"Mama, Mama. Aleck. Look! *Look!* Only see what I have. See my presents."

"Binnie girl, please. Try to show some respect for the Sabbath. You can behave with decorum *one* day a week."

The sight of the gifts caused Mrs. Howe to check her scolding, and Binnie's obvious pleasure led her to smile back —though reluctantly—at Binnie.

"That *was* nice of Maria. Are they for you to keep? She must have spent a lot of money on those. 'Course, it's easier for her than for some," Mama observed.

True. Maria did not have to budget her monies very closely. Unlike the others, she never had to send any of her wages home. In fact, her rich merchant father often sent her gifts of silk, money and perfume. It crossed Binnie's mind that the most costly present for Maria to give would be some of her precious time and independence. Impatiently, Binnie pushed away the thought. She refused to let any words of Mama's or thoughts of her own dim the joy of today.

Binnie stroked the smooth leather of her book. Carefully, she wrapped the tissue around the two again and stood on the ladder-back chair. Then she stretched to put her parcel up on the top of the wardrobe where she kept her *Aesop's Fables*. It was a safe place, too high for Aleck's grubby hands to reach.

"Binnie, c'n I see? Let me touch, too."

"No. Later."

"Where y'going? Can I go with you? Aren't you going to read your new book?"

"*No*. And double no," Binnie answered Aleck as she headed into the kitchen.

She stuffed some cold corn pone into her pockets. Before he could raise his voice in protest, she was gone—out of the house and moving down the street. Binnie had put off reading her book purposely. By not gobbling it in a single day, the joy would last longer. Maybe she would take a whole week to read the book and each day that she picked it up would renew the pleasure of this day.

Overhead, two black crows wheeled and cawed noisily. Binnie looked up at them and laughed. She was convinced that with a couple of deep breaths, she could be up there flying with them. Her feet skimmed the dusty path and sent puffs of dirt up behind her heels. Crossing Lowell Street, she slowed to a trot that was half her earlier speed and almost ladylike. She felt puffed up, her skin stretched to bursting with self-importance.

If she saw that boy, that Packy . . . if he happened to

walk by, she would hail him and tell him about her presents. Binnie thought, too, of turning down the hard-packed uneven dirt street that led into the heart of the Acre but her nerve failed her. She skirted the edge of the shantytown, moving slower than a tortoise and throwing quick nervous looks over her right shoulder.

For all the hundreds and hundreds of Irishers who lived there packed together, the scene was remarkably unpeopled. A lone fat woman carrying a linen-covered basket, two men greeting one another with a clap on the shoulders, a little girl in ninepenny calico skipping out of sight into an alley.

The street curved, bent and disappeared into a jumble of squat cabins turfed to the eaves, tents, shacks of rough slab boards—all barely a body's width apart. Everyone said the Acre was a blot on the landscape, a sin against decency. But the weathered gray of unpainted boards shone silver in the sun, and to Binnie's eyes, it looked a cozy place, almost beautiful.

Where was that Packy McCabe? Binnie threw one last look back at the shantytown and reluctantly settled on a goal. She zigged and zagged her way across open meadows to Pawtucket Falls. The grand roar and splash of the falls would suit her present mood.

In the end, she met Packy as she always had, by running right into him. The rushing waters that fell from the slatey cliffs masked her approach. She slid down the banks to the river where he was standing. The scatter of pebbles falling at his feet took him by surprise.

"Wo-oof." His let-out breath sounded like a bark.

He had just pulled his braided belt tight in a knot and his

hands stopped dead with the belt ends held up in the air. His black hair was soaked flat against his scalp and framed a perfectly square head. After blinking in surprise, he glared at her. Clearly, he had only this moment finished pulling on his pants.

Of course. He had been swimming—not where the boys and men from town went but down here where it was sheltered from sight, the waters still, the river bed free from potholes. Binnie had paddled here in her shimmy when she was the age of Aleck.

"Hang you, Binnie. Don't you ever just walk? You go like a steam engine everywhere and you're likely to blow yourself up."

Binnie smothered her smile. Anybody would be flustered at almost being caught naked.

"Seeing as it's my Birth Day, I figured I'm welcome." She shrugged and boldly made a face at him. "I don't see you these days. I just came by where you live," she added.

"My uncle's come to live with us. We're moved from the Acre. Do you know the soap works? Mead's on Union Street between Charles and North? We're right next to that but one house removed. It's a grand big house with six rooms. And two floors."

Binnie thought hard. She realized suddenly which one he meant and was startled. The tall house was a narrow, mean-looking place with only two windows in the front. It had stood empty for some years. Few people liked to rent near the soap factory because of the strong, foul smells it produced. Maybe if you came from one of those squat window-less sheds . . . maybe then a person would think the ramshackle frame house with a second story was grand and spacious. She nodded cautiously to show him she knew which one he meant.

"My mother hopes to board the schoolmaster, but my uncle knows some men from the canal boats who are tired of Barron's Hotel and looking to board. Either way, we'll have somebody paying in."

"That's good. Does she still think to have you go to the high school?"

"Yeah. But, I think my uncle can bring her around soon to letting me work." He was smiling now, cheerful.

He led the way out to the flat rock on the point of land, and Binnie followed him. Sitting in the sun, they had a good view of Pawtucket Falls and the traffic on the river. The fishermen had long gone from the sandy islet in the middle, but a father and son poled their way downstream in a canoe. Binnie offered him some cold corn pone and he nodded thanks as he took a chunk. She scooped handfuls of cold clear water to drink and used one last handful to wash the gritty corn bread crumbs from her face.

"So it's your Birth Day." Packy had come back to their starting point.

Now that she had his full attention, Binnie sailed into a full telling of what this day had brought.

"That's what Maria said and this is the best day I ever had in my whole life," she finished in a rush.

"I can see that." He grinned at her. "So this Patrick person and you share the same Birth Day? And he was a big hero? H-mmm." Packy rubbed his nose with one finger and his blue eyes stared hard at Binnie. "Makes you kind of think that you're bound to be someone special, too, in some way, doesn't it?" he said thoughtfully.

Exactly. He had pulled the plum out of the pudding that was this special day. How many people could claim to be linked in any way with a hero?

"I guess you had better believe that you're going to win glory, Miss Skinny Binnie. You'll have to start growing, though . . . enough so that people can see you when you step out in front of the crowd." He laughed.

Binnie didn't mind the teasing about her size. Not when he confirmed her feeling that she stood on the edge of something important that would last her all of her life. Packy brushed his hands off on the side of his already dirty pants.

"I don't recollect too much about him from my history. Say, when you finish with it, can I read your book?"

"Sure enough. After I finish."

Binnie's grin split her face. Already she was an important person. She and she alone had something that Packy Mc-Cabe wanted. Binnie was struck by a new idea. He himself must have answers to some questions that had puzzled her for a long time. With her newfound confidence, she asked him. Was it true that the Pope talked with the Devil every day? Did he really claim more power than the President of the United States?

Patrick dismissed the whole with a casual wave. "Somebody's gotta be boss and that's what he is, a boss. Just like an overseer for the souls of the priests and the people. Back there when you were saying stuff about heroes and the Revolution, you reminded me . . . ," said Packy. He went on to brag about his grandfa'r, a soldier in the Revolution who had fought with Lafayette.

Binnie allowed him his brag, then went on to boast about her own grandfather, the sea captain who had sailed around the bottom of South America.

They sat, soaking up sun and talking, the whole afternoon. At the end of the day, they walked home slowly, stopping once to pick some ripe strawberries in Osgood's meadow. He left her at the edge of the boarding house row with a final teasing.

"Don't forget. Let me know when you make your first million dollars."

Binnie walked into the house with a happy, satisfied feeling that carried into the dull, even days that followed. Mrs. Howe was slowly picking up her usual tasks, so Binnie again had some free moments. She read very little and used the extra time for money-earning jobs.

One day she scoured the countryside and her house for empty bottles and phials. The apothecary paid six and a half cents for every dozen brought to him. Another day she devoted to tasks for Granny Anna Folger, although Granny Anna was a less certain source of money. Sometimes she pretended that Binnie came to work out of pure neighborly love; sometimes she paid for the chores that were done. Mostly it depended on the state of the old lady's temper on that particular day. She greeted Binnie this day with her cackling laugh that showed toothless red gums.

"Come to make yourself useful to an old lady, huh? That Canuck rooster is only good for yard work and he don't do all of that, either. He can't touch my cow. She kicks and runs away whenever she smells a man." Granny laughed so hard that she coughed, wheezed and finally had to spit in order to recover. "I'm way behind, too, with my 'broideries. You want to sort the wools and set some needles up for me," she told Binnie.

Binnie sorted out yarns by color and threaded needles. Granny's milky eye could not see well enough to do that herself. That same cloudy eye explained why Granny's finished work sometimes contained the most startling combinations of colors. Binnie went steadily from one chore to another: stripping dried leaves from the bunches of plants and herbs, grinding berries to a grainy powder, stringing dried blossoms.

When she went home, she had another fourpence to add to the pile in the handkerchief behind the mantel clock. Binnie tried to picture a plump money bag, so big and full that it spilled out from behind the pillar-and-scroll clock. She gave a defeated sigh. The hoard grew with such painful slowness, she would be older than Granny Anna before it came about.

Mrs. Howe startled Binnie by calling her to come to the bedroom. "Where have you been? Botheration, Binnie, I've been waiting. Come quickly."

Binnie found her mother lying on the bed in her chemise and a small feather of fear tickled her. But Mrs. Howe sounded more cross than sick as she turned over to lie face down.

"You know, that cold is still seated upon my lungs and I have a dreadful ache in the small of my back. I want you to give me a good walk down my back and rub some liniment there after. Hurry up, but wipe your feet first."

Binnie did as she was told. She enjoyed giving her

mother a massage, partly because she was the only one permitted to do it. Mrs. Howe went on talking although her voice was muffled by the bedclothes.

"Grace Little got a letter. She says there's been two cases of cholera already in Springfield. They do say a hot May makes a fat graveyard. *Ummph.*" She grunted as Binnie stepped on the sore spot by the kidney. She murmured a grateful "oh-hh, that feels good" as Binnie reached the shoulder blades. Back and forth Binnie stepped delicately up and down her mother's back. She rubbed in liniment until her arms ached and her mother said thank you. Her mother sat up to slip her dress over her head. When her head reappeared, she spoke abruptly, almost angrily.

"I wrote to Cornelia. Cornelia Howe that's married to your papa's first cousin down New Bedford way. She's asked for an age now to take Aleck. I've decided he's to go just for the summer. The sea breezes will be good for him."

Binnie's eyebrow lifted up and her mouth made an oval of surprise. Send Aleck away to New Bedford simply because miles and miles west of Lowell someone had caught cholera? Surely that was inviting trouble in and hugging it to your bosom. Still, if she was willing to part with Aleck, she must be truly worried.

"I fear a little child .... Aleck has never ... well, just look at *me*. One little sickness and I am forever about getting over it."

Mrs. Howe headed for the kitchen, speaking briskly, as she moved. "Regardless, it'll do him good to change. The seashore has clean dirt at least and healthy waters. Not like this noisy city with its tainted air and all the noxious dyes and bleaches always pouring into the waters.... Since he goes alone, I'm sending him by the railroad, and Mr. Howe will meet him in the Boston depot. We must get his clothes ready. No son of mine goes away looking like an orphan," she finished fiercely.

Binnie felt envy rising up like a sour burp in her throat. Aleck would get new clothes and a trip to Boston plus the treat of a ride on the railroad. Binnie could not think of anyone she knew who had ridden on a train. Even Adam had traveled by way of the Middlesex Canal on the slow-moving boat that took all day to reach Boston. Lucky duck Aleck.

More than once in the next week she choked with resentment as well as envy. Aleck strutted, crowed and generously invited the women to pat and hug him. Pointing out that he would soon be gone, he accepted their gifts of candy and odd pennies graciously.

On his last night at home, he told Binnie that she had to take him out to the necessary. The pulse-stopping sounds of mice and insects scuttling up the walls in the dark scared him. Binnie rebelled flatly.

"Go and do your own bum! By yourself!" She added spitefully, "Anybody big enough to go to Boston has to be able to visit an outhouse by himself—or he can't go away."

The warning reached him and he went off with trembling lower lip instead of the temper tantrum that she expected. Binnie squashed her feeling of guilt by thinking of his pockets bulging with candy and presents.

On the summer schedule, three trains left Lowell every day for Boston and Aleck was to leave on the afternoon one. The station stood on the corner of Merrimack and Dutton streets, a five-minute walk from the house. A crowd had collected early for the two P.M. train. Some came to make the trip, some for the excitement of watching the departure. Even though the trains had been running for a full year, the fascination of the monster locomotives belching in and out of the station had not faded. Mrs. Howe entered the impressive portico on Merrimack. Binnie and Aleck stepped around to the flanking train shed.

At the sight of the train, Aleck hesitated and hung back. Binnie tugged at his hand and reminded him that he was a lucky boy.

"Is it the longest train in all the country, Binnie?"

"May well be. Count the cars and we'll see."

Aleck inched forward to see the end car and moved his lips. He counted forward up to the engine and Binnie counted with him. Nine all together. The flatbed freight cars carried finished cotton cloth lashed and covered with canvas. The passenger cars, looking very much like stagecoaches, had room for six people each. Up front, the engine had huge wheels bigger than any wagon she had ever seen. The boiler painted with bright stripes made rumbling, thunderlike noises.

"See!" Binnie called, pointing to the seven-foot-high smokestack. "That's why they call it 'teakettle-on-a-track.' "

Aleck laughed. The engineer was ringing the bell vigorously, calling the passengers to get on. At the sound, Aleck shied nervously, like a frightened horse. Mrs. Howe and the conductor who had sold the tickets inside the depot both reached the children at the same time.

"I'll see that his bag gets off with him at Boston, ma'am." the conductor promised. He peeled a now terrified Aleck from Binnie's side and swung him into the nearest coach.

"Ma-a-ma. I want my mama."

Through the train noise, Binnie could hear Aleck wailing. He was trying to push his way back out but the only woman there tugged him back. She sat him down firmly in her lap and wrapped her arms around to hold him. His tearstained face tilted up and turned from side to side, hunting for Mrs. Howe and Binnie. The handsome cap, new for the trip, barely rested on the back of his head. A card lettered with his name and Cousin Cornelia's address hung on a stout cord around his neck, and with all his squirming it had slipped up behind his ear. He looked for all the world like a badly wrapped package addressed for delivery, Binnie thought.

Good thing Mama had pinned still another card inside on his underwear. What if the outside card got torn off? Would the "package" still be delivered? And what if no one claimed the parcel arriving on the afternoon train? The tears flooding her eyes surprised her. She had been prepared to feel relief, not this sudden fear and sadness.

The conductor blew his whistle, signaling the engineer to start. Binnie stood on tiptoe, suddenly frantic for a last look. The lady in the coach had offered Aleck her reticule to explore. His head down now, he was looking through the contents of the bag. Mrs. Howe turned her back as soon as Aleck's coach passed, but Binnie waved good-by as hard and as long as she could.

"Do you mean to stand there gawking all day? There's work at home waiting for us and it won't get done by us standing here. Let's go quickly."

Mrs. Howe's voice sounded loud and angry and she set off abruptly down Merrimack. Binnie saw her mother's hand stuff a handkerchief into the pocket under her apron. Her crumpled face as she turned away had looked the twin of

Aleck's, tearstains and all. Mrs. Howe's face and voice made it plain that she did not want either company or comments.

Just as well. Binnie had her own demons of gloom to wrestle away. The days ahead promised to hold more of the same. Dull, dreary days of chores exactly like her other summer days. Only Aleck would be missing from her list of Obligations.

Only Aleck? Most of all, Aleck. A sudden realization hit Binnie and made the hairs on the back of her neck prickle. Dear God, how could she have missed the importance of that change? It made all the difference in her world.

Charged with excitement, Binnie started sprinting and almost passed Mrs. Howe. She forced herself to slow and fall back again. She did not want to be in front of her mother just now. Sometimes she had the feeling that Mama could see inside her head and Binnie was not yet ready. She needed time to examine the new hope. She needed time to arrange her arguments and she needed time to practice them. Maybe Patrick Henry could stand up on the spot and persuade people with the eloquence of his words. But Arabinia J. Howe was not Patrick Henry.

Yet ... if she chose her words with care, reason was on her side. Binnie vowed she would persuade her mother. And she would do it before another week passed.

8

"Pay-day . . . . bee-yoo-ti-ful, beeyoutiful pay-ay-day."

Florilla Nappet's caroling and the great whinnying laugh which followed could be heard clearly out in the kitchen. Binnie grinned to herself. Singing at the table might not be ladylike, but it certainly expressed how all the women felt about the day. As she flew in and out of the dining room with the platters and plates, she thought again about her plan. Tomorrow. Perhaps, tomorrow after her mother finished her Bible reading, she would be in the best humor to be approached.

"Are you settled on what you're buying this week?" Dorcas asked Phoebe Little.

"Nothing. I'm not buying anything. This was only a four-week pay period. I have to pay my quarterly pew rent and make my contribution to the Missionary Offering. Those are all the extras I can manage this time. I do wish, though, that we got our money every week instead of once a month."

"Well, if you'd stop sending so much to that nephew of yours for his mortgage, you'd be better off. Take care of your own self, I always say." Dorcas shrugged. "I could have kissed the paymaster today when I saw him with that money box. I've been so afraid that the Highland shawls would all be gone from Homer and Peabody's. And I mean to have new horn combs from Elliot's."

"You are too ready to kiss more than the paymaster and with less excuse," said Phoebe sharply.

"Just what do you think to accuse me of?" An angry Dorcas pushed her plate away. Big red blotches appeared in her white skin.

In the sudden silence, everyone heard the banging on the front door. As Mrs. Howe opened it, the high tenor voice of an angry man could be heard. Mrs. Howe backed up and the tall man who was advancing into the front hall became visible to the watching women. The silence was absolute as they gaped at him. A handsome man running to fat, he had the blurred outline of a tallow candle melting down.

"I want to see my wife, Harriet Stanton." He was smiling a loose, sloppy smile that somehow looked mean.

"Mr.— Sir, as I told you at the door, we have no Mrs. Stanton here."

"That's right. She's a cunning, sly fox. Harriet Smith she calls herself now. They told me over to the countinghouse she lodges here." His eyes swept the room, looking from face to face.

The mouse? The mouse was married to this man? And had lied about herself? Binnie could hardly believe it.

"I don't see her. *The lady, Harriet Smith*," Mrs. Howe said with delicate emphasis and a tight mouth, "does not seem to have come down for this meal, sir. I shall see if she is in her room."

Binnie could tell Mama was furious, but at which one? Harriet Smith for disguising herself? Or at him for barging and banging his way into the house? Binnie could not decide.

He had an air of satisfaction about him as he explained to

the watching women: "I lay sick on my bed when she run away. A bold piece she's always been, always wanting money and more money. She saw her chance and left me when I was down. But I knew I could find her soon as I put my mind to it."

Binnie decided he was lying beyond any possible belief. Whatever the mouse was, she was not bold.

"There's no one in her room Mr.—uh . . . Stanton. She's not there. Nor are her belongings there." Mrs. Howe had come back quietly. She sounded to Binnie's ears as if she had found exactly what she had expected to find.

"What d'y' mean? The overseer at the mill knew who I wanted and said she left sick in the middle of the day. I was watching by the gates, but she must have sneaked past me. Her stuff has to be here. They give me her wages for this month but I want my money from the weeks before, too."

Mrs. Howe, who was too short to look over his head, fixed her eyes on a point beyond his right shoulder and said, "You must find your wife and settle your business with her, sir. She's not here and we cannot help you further."

"Says you. I wanna go up and look for myself. Her wages is mine by law, you know, and everything she owns, too. I'm entitled and I want what's mine. When I get ahold of her, I'll . . . . Where did she sleep?"

"Binnie, show Mr. Stanton upstairs. It needs but a moment to see for yourself. No longer. We have much to do here and I cannot permit you to disrupt the affairs of my other lodgers."

Binnie slipped around Stanton and started up the stairs. She listened to him wheeze behind her and caught a strong whiff of rum with each wheeze. Silently, she pointed out the mouse's corner of the room. It was completely empty with only a cleaning rag hung on the peg by her side of the bed. He cursed. A steady stream of foul words spat like tobacco juice out of his mouth.

"You forget yourself in front of the girl." Grace Little spoke sharply from behind Binnie. "I share the other corner and I wish to use my room, sir. Mrs. Howe is waiting for you."

The man muttered and lurched out of the room with Binnie following on his heels. Downstairs he spoke in an ugly voice to Mrs. Howe.

"I'm holding you responsible. You must have seen her, you must know where she is. Did she give you her bank book to hold for her?"

"She's gone and *we* don't know where she is. Speak to the authorities if you are *truly* concerned about your wife's welfare," Mrs. Howe snapped back and opened the front door. "Leave, sir."

Binnie gasped. She thought for one moment that the big man was going to swing at her mother. Mrs Howe did not flinch, only stood straight and waiting by the open door.

"I'll do that. I'll just talk to the authorities. That money's mine. I'll have the law on her for taking off with it. That's what I'll do." He left, shutting the door with a bang.

"Well .... Did you ever? ... I can't believe .... " A storm of shocked exclamations filled the room.

"Yes, but you know there's no mistaking that Harriet for somebody else. She has that big mole on her chin. No wonder they believed him and gave him her wages," said Grace.

Maria spoke for once with passionate feeling. "The law

. . . my foot! There ought to be a law against men like him. If a woman doesn't have any family to protect or help her stand against . . . . That poor soul!"

Binnie agreed. It was the mouse who had worked and worked hard for the money. Why should the paymaster turn it over to the husband? It was scarcely different from being a slave if everything you earned got turned over to somebody else.

"He was a handsome one, though, wasn't he? What'd he ever see in her? Don't you 'spose he could have better than the mouse?"

"Oh, Dorcas, how *can* you say that? I imagine that's exactly how she got trapped, thinking she was lucky to catch such a fellow. I can just guess what kind of 'sickness' he had. That man was a pig, a drunken sot," Maria answered.

"Harriet Smith had black and blues the whole of her back and her legs, too, when she come here." The widow Penfield spoke sternly to Porky-Dorky while her eyes said something in silent signal to Mrs. Howe.

Binnie caught that look and realized suddenly that a number of people in the house had not been surprised by the turn of events.

Later, Binnie found her mother in the kitchen and asked: Had she truly not seen Harriet Smith sneak away in the middle of the afternoon? Where had the woman gone? What had it all meant?

"What it means is that we have one less paying boarder and, consequently, less money. That's what it all means," Mrs. Howe answered wryly.

Binnie noticed that she had sidestepped the first questions. Her mother's remark, however, gave her the perfect opening. *Now*, thought Binnie, and she plunged into her argument, delivering it all in one breath.

"If we need more money, Mama, you know I'm twelve now. Aleck is gone and I can do it with no trouble. I can be a doffer and even come home between times so I'll still be helping you here."

"Not tonight, Binnie. Why do you bring that up when you know how I feel about girls in the mill? I can't make any decisions now. Maybe later."

"Please say yes, Mama. Please, please. It would help you, and I so much want to do it. The corporations require only three months to be used for schooling each year and I've already done that much, so I'm free to start and stay on in the mill. Please, Mama, please."

She was pleading hard now, hoping to overcome her mother's objections by a flood of words instead of just a choice few.

"Binnie, don't tease me any more for an answer or you'll be sorry. And don't cry, either. I've helped wipe enough tears today to float a cow." Mrs. Howe flapped her hands as if to shoo away a buzzing bluebottle fly. "Go get that table cleared off. Be sure there's no crumbs left. Florilla means to cut out a dress on it tonight."

Binnie went sullenly. If only she had not cared so much, if only she had been able to measure out her words slowly . . . . In the other room, Porky-Dorky and Florilla were arguing.

"You can't just cut that like a flour sack with two arm-holes and another for the neck."

"I can't do but plain sewing, Dorcas. I leave all the la-di-da Boston notions to them that can work out fancy patterns,"

94

Florilla protested with an edge to her good-natured voice.

"You have a fine long neck and a good bosom that would show to advantage in the new wider neckline. Besides that, with a gigot-style sleeve your waist will look less thick."

What a silly argument, Binnie thought. It was Florilla's cloth. Why couldn't she do what she pleased with it? Porky-Dorky had no business messing with it.

Dorcas continued, her eyes narrowed in a calculating look.

"Tell you what. Let me cut and pin it and I promise you that the stitching of it will all be plain and simple," she offered.

"But you were going out upon the street tonight to shop. And I can't pay you for your services," Florilla said weakly. She recognized that the battle was lost.

"I'll go later or another time," Dorcas answered. "I don't want any pay. After all, we're workmates, aren't we? If we don't help one another out, who will? Anyway," she finished with blunt honesty, "it pains me too much to see you abuse a fine piece of goods. That's what you'll do: abuse, not use it. I can't bear that."

Binnie shook her head in wonder. Only Dorcas Boomer could make a melodrama out of what happened to a piece of cloth. The thought of Dorcas giving up her beloved shopping put Binnie back into a good humor and she left the room still shaking her head but grinning.

For the next few days, Binnie grinned often. With no Aleck to watch over, suddenly she had time to spare. But, to her growing dismay, she found, too, that she had nothing else to do. For the moment, she had come to an end of books borrowed from friends and chores for pay. One fine day followed another, but Binnie's good spirits slowly waned in the boredom that filled each day.

On the sunniest, brightest day yet, a restless Binnie flung herself out of the house. She roamed aimlessly across fields lavishly spread with buttercups and scented with clover. The May smell of lilacs and apple blossoms had already been replaced by June's heavier, sweeter smell of wild roses and honeysuckle. The rude plants—as Granny Anna called the nettles, thistles and burdocks—had thrust themselves up under fences and around corner posts. Summer had settled in.

Binnie flopped down and lay flat in the grass, waiting. She was waiting for the irritation and discontent to ooze away. Once, long ago, she had seen a rowboat up on blocks in a farmer's haying meadow. Sitting in that impossible place, it had made a lasting impression on her. She felt now like that rowboat: beached high and dry with no place to go and no way to get there, empty and waiting.

Reaching out to the side, she idly picked some burrs. Then she sat up to reach deeper into the stalks for still more. She stuck one spiny burr to another and the mass took on the faint shape of a building. If she built it up a little higher and roofed it, the whole would make a splendid livery stable.

Suddenly Binnie grabbed the hollow ball of burrs and tossed them aside angrily. Why bother? Aleck wasn't here to play stable boy and sweep it out with a broom of pine needles. There was no point to pretending, no point to turning Queen Anne's lace into a fairy's table. No more milkweed milk in acorn cups, no more pumpkin pies of brown daisy centers. She felt too silly at her age to play make-believe for herself alone. When Aleck left, he had taken the last of her childhood with him as surely as if he had packed it in his carpetbag. Regret stung Binnie with more pain than the prickly burrs had.

Far off, she heard the end-of-the-day bells ringing in an uneven ragged chorus. Even if she wanted the satisfaction of a good hard cry, there was no longer time for one.

At home, Binnie's dismal face attracted only Florilla's attention.

"Hey, Binnie, what's gnawing at your liver?" she asked.

"Nothing. I hate my age. I wish I was already grown up, that's all," she blurted and turned her back to go into the kitchen.

"Don't you know that the fastest growing pumpkin always turns out the poorest? At least that's what our farmers to home say," Florilla called out to her in consolation.

Binnie glanced at her mother to see if she had noticed her daughter's misery. Maybe if she squeezed out a tear? Mrs. Howe looked at Binnie with a frown, but her eyes were not seeing her.

"We got a letter from Adam."

The letter did not seem to have given her the pleasure that she usually got from her older son's writings.

"The Reverend Hall has agreed to tutor him especially. They'll be going to the White Mountains for a spell, maybe a month or more. It's a wonderful opportunity to do botany with a true naturalist." Her mother stopped, pushed back the wisps of limp hair falling on her forehead and said, "Of course, it means he'll not be earning any money this summer and where I'll get . . . ." She had stopped short again. "Well, don't dawdle, girl. The women want their supper."

Out in the dining room an argument had broken out that was swamping all other conversation.

"I tell you it's true. The girls at Tremont swear the overseers are putting the clocks back every afternoon to get more work out of them."

"I don't believe that the company would do anything so dishonorable."

"When it comes to profit, they'll do anything to boost it," said Dorcas knowingly.

"And why shouldn't they?" the widow asked. "After all, the directors have put their money into the corporations for the purpose of making money."

"If it's so, we have only ourselves to blame," said Grace Little. "When women get to the gates well before the bells ring and beg to have them opened early because they are so eager to earn extra, then the agents cannot be faulted for believing that we are all willing to go for extra hours."

"Absurd. Fourteen hours is enough for any body to endure in that place. Those who want to earn more can speed up themselves," said Maria. "Anyone who moves with dispatch can increase the total of pieces to her credit without adding to others' hours."

"I agree with you, Maria," said Mrs. Howe. "I understand that someone who is naturally fast, like Binnie, makes the best kind of factory worker."

"Do you think to have Binnie join us soon?" asked Maria.

"Sooner or later, I suppose. A poor widow must use every resource to care for her family and it seems foolish to overlook the opportunity at hand. I know the factory needs help badly in the summer. Now may be as good a time as any to earn a little extra."

Binnie had been hungrily eyeing the bowls full of fresh, sweet garden peas making the rounds of the table, but her attention snapped back now to the conversation. Mama sounded as if she had about talked herself into letting Binnie work. Could she perhaps pin Mama down? Get her to name a day in front of the women?

"When, Mama? What day are we going to the corporation?"

Mrs. Howe gave Binnie a look that said she understood too well her purpose. Still, she answered promptly. "This week, so you can be on the payroll before the first of July."

Binnie was so stunned that she almost dropped the bowls that had finally come into her hands, but she knew better than to say another word. She carried the peas out to the kitchen and strained to hear what else might be said in the dining room.

"Sugar is so dear now. And you just can't use sorghum molasses for so many things."

Binnie guessed that her mother was passing out the strawberry-rhubarb pies. Those tart pies made only in June used cups and cups of sugar hacked off the big, costly cone in the pantry. Aha! Binnie snapped her fingers. A fig for the cost. With Binnie's earnings coming into the house, Mama could make dozens and dozens of the pies and never think about the expense. She twirled around once and hugged herself in delight.

The morning they set out for the countinghouse, a very quiet Binnie walked close to her mother's side. Another scrap of conversation from that night had come back to her.

". . . Not to worry, Mrs. Howe. At least our bosses don't practice the wretched cruelties of the English system on the children."

Too late now to ask why it had been said. Or what those

unnamed cruelties might be. Already they were at the door of the long brick countinghouse. No visitor could enter the mill without stopping here first for a pass. In this building all the hiring, firing, bargains and business of the mill took place. As she entered, Binnie sucked in her stomach and pushed back her shoulders. She wanted to look as tall and old as possible.

"Mr. Quimby. Sir, may I speak with you?"

The man Mrs. Howe had approached was himself not very tall. Even so, no one could overlook him. He had a great thick mane of waving hair that rippled, tossed and moved with his every breath. His long, ruler-straight nose hung down over his top lip. It made him look like the plaster bust of some Roman emperor, dignified but disagreeable.

Mrs. Howe presented Binnie to him, explaining that this was her own daughter, ready for employment. If he would be so kind as to consider her for a position, he would find her a good, hard-working child. To Binnie, her mother's voice sounded softer than usual and oddly hesitant. Especially by contrast with Franklin Quimby, whose answering voice was round, full and juicy like a dark purple plum.

"Well, well, Mrs. Howe. No need. No need to establish her merits with me. Your credit at the Merrimack is good. I know you and I know that anyone you bring is virtuous and industrious. You know me well, too. I am always happy to help our young people attain to a higher moral condition by enlisting them in our little company of workers."

"I have here her school certificate from the last spring session of this year." Mrs. Howe was fumbling in her pocket.

He waved away the need to read it.

"Yes, indeed, Mrs. Howe. Children need gainful work,

need to learn the value of money and the value of work for its own sake. They incline by nature toward the Devil's work, unfortunately. Give them but a moment of their own, let them run free and they get into trouble. You're right to bring her here."

A small bullet of anger exploded inside Binnie. How could this preachy man judge her so out of hand? She wanted to tell him about her painfully earned coppers, proof that he had been unfair.

"I do believe, as the Bible tells us, that the laborer is worthy of his hire," Mrs. Howe answered him indirectly and pulled Binnie in closer to her side.

The voices droned on, settling details. "She'll need clogs to keep safe her . . . ."

Mama's swift look down told Binnie that it was a mistake to have come barefoot. Binnie curled her toes under to make the bareness less visible.

Finally it was done. She stood on an empty bobbin box and signed the Regulation Papers. This was her contract of employment, but she had no time to read all the promises and requirements in it. Only the bottom line stood out: a promise on her part to "regular attendance" at some place of worship. Binnie was disappointed. She had thought there would be more to mark the beginning of her employment, some ceremony.

The buying of clogs was done just as speedily. Down on Central Street, they found a sample pair on display. Thick black leather nailed onto a thick wooden sole. The soles were bound with iron edges. The shape always reminded Binnie of a horseshoe. To make them look more inviting and daintier, these samples had been cobbled extra small and narrow.

They fit Binnie better than Mama had expected, and Binnie insisted on wearing them home.

"Might as well get used to them," her mother agreed reluctantly.

Stiff and hard, the clogs made loud clumping noises on the attic stairs as Binnie hurried to show them to Florilla and Maria.

"By gravy, Binnie, they look like doll's shoes," Florilla exclaimed.

"Not so small as that," Binnie argued, stepping next to Maria and measuring foot to foot with her.

"Well, they surely do when you look at mine. Canal boats, that's what I have to wear. Now Maria's foot looks like a lady's still."

Florilla, who had put her own foot next to the others, was laughing at the comparison. Standing twelve, fourteen hours a day, walking back and forth tending the drawing frames and looms made everyone's feet spread out; some, like Florilla, wore men's shoes for comfort.

"Mine have grown one full size longer this year," Maria complained with a frown. Despite her complaint, she still had shapely feet: narrow, high-arched, with smooth skin and straight, delicate-looking toes.

"I *want* mine to grow," Binnie announced. Her own feet were slim and free from ugly bunions and corns. In this much, at least, she was very like Maria. If her feet grew even a little, a part of her old ambition—to look like Maria Teasdale—was bound to come true.

All the past year when Binnie had longed to work in the mill, she had not thought much about what went on *inside* the handsome brick walls. She understood dimly that powerful machines tended by women spun the thread and wove cloth, but exactly how machines and women worked together was unclear. She felt a stir of anticipation at the prospect of finding out how it was done.

Mr. Quimby had instructed her to report to Spinning Room Number 2, which was in the middle building in the yard. Binnie did her morning chores as usual, which meant she left the house later than the boarders. Although she raced to catch up, they had already passed out of sight.

She was unprepared for the great crush of bodies jostling through the gates at the mill yard. The crowd squeezed and hustled her up the stairway at the side of the mill faster than she wanted to go. She was swept into a large bright room that filled rapidly with women. Fifty? Sixty? Binnie lost count. All the women moved mysteriously but purposefully up to the rows of machines. Three or four men walked down the alleys, stopping here and there to tug or tighten something on the spinning frames. One of these men told Binnie to stand down at the end of the room until he had time to deal with her.

"Keep your eyes skinned and be ready to jump smart when told," he advised.

Binnie scuttled to the far end and tried to look alert and intelligent. The room before her had some homely touches that cheered her. The window sills were crowded with geraniums and other pots of flowering plants. The floor was painted green, which added to the cheerful look.

Hers was now the only figure not moving in the huge room. Fright and nervousness made Binnie crack the knuckles in her fingers. The cracking sounded loud to her, but no one looked at Binnie.

From somewhere deep in the bowels of the mill, a rumbling started and grew instantly loud. The whole mill seemed to shake itself alive. Under her feet, the wooden floor shook with regular rhythmic thumps. Over her head, giant leather belts creaked and groaned around wooden pulleys as metal gears clicked and clanked. The power had been connected.

Binnie was half-stupefied by roaring noises that swirled into the very bones of her body. She saw people's lips moving but no words seeped through the din. A nightmare thought struck her. How could she learn what she was to do if she couldn't hear the overseer's instructions?

When he did speak to her through lips placed carefully close to her ear, the words—throstle, warp, roving—were alien and meaningless to Binnie. She did grasp that for these first morning hours she was simply to follow the other doffers around. There seemed to be a pair of doffers for every nine or ten spinners, but where the dividing lines were for each one's section she could not tell. By observing the others, she would learn her duties, he indicated. Binnie's relief that she had nothing more to do than watch and follow was short-lived.

Susan, a plump young girl whom she remembered from school last year, moved swiftly past her. Carrying a box of bobbins, Susan raced to a spinning frame, halfway down the room. Even as Binnie realized that the frame was stopped and before she could start after Susan, the job was done. Susan's flying hands had replaced the fully wound bobbins with empties and she had started back. Binnie, who prided herself on her speed, was stung with jealousy and shame.

She was more ready the next time she saw a doffer move, but still her own moves came a fraction too late. Where the experienced doffers slipped easily through the rows of big noisy spinning frames, Binnie edged awkwardly and fearfully. She felt clumsy, slow and stupid. When the first of the day's dismissal bells rang, Binnie was too afraid of doing the wrong thing to move quickly. She was almost the last to leave the room.

Speed was important at home, too, but there she felt comfortable doing what she always had. She snatched some cold pudding for her own breakfast before going out with platters of food for the boarders. To every question about the work, Binnie answered with a quick "All right, I guess." The bells ringing put an abrupt end to both the meal and the conversations. There was no free time left. Hastily, Binnie stuffed a hard chunk of bread into her pocket. As she headed back to the mill, she gnawed on a smaller chunk.

Inside the gates, she dodged around a flatbed wagon loaded with bales of cotton. Two men with begrimed faces were wheeling it across the yard to the picker house. Binnie, looking back over her shoulder, realized suddenly that the men were Mary Kate's brothers. Mary Kate had said they worked at the dirtiest and most unsafe job: opening the bales of cotton and preparing the cotton for carding. Fires broke out frequently in the picker house for some reason that Mary Kate couldn't explain. The danger had something to do with cotton dust and the rapidly moving machine parts.

Dorcas, who had come up behind Binnie, tugged at her to keep moving. They climbed the stairs together but Dorcas continued up the next flight to the weavers' room while Binnie turned into the spinning room.

By the noon dinner break, Binnie had sorted out some of what was going on around her. Somewhere downstairs, out of sight, the raw cotton was combed, cleaned, twisted, stretched and doubled on itself to make a loose rope called "roving." An elevator, a large creaky platform hoisted by ropes, carried these boxes of roving up to the spinning room. It was one overseer's job to keep count and measure out roving. On the spinning frames, called "throstles," hundreds and hundreds of spindles whirled around in a mad dance as the loose rope changed into strong coarse yarn. After that, the yarn disappeared onto the upper floors to be dressed and wound on beams for the weavers' looms.

Binnie's newly won confidence slipped when a spinner whose frame had not stopped beckoned her to come. The woman spoke, but Binnie could not make out a word over the buzzing of the spindles. She stared mute and round eyed as the woman pointed at her head and made grabbing, yanking motions. Finally, the woman hunted in her apron pocket, pulled out a piece of string and reached for Binnie's braids. She wrapped the two braids around Binnie's head and tied them together with the string. With a smile and a wave, she dismissed Binnie and the girl, still puzzled, walked away.

Minutes later she was struck with understanding, an understanding followed swiftly by horror.

"Bind your hair," the woman had been saying. "Bind your hair." The turning gears, the whirring wheels, the flying spindles that devoured roving would just as easily snatch a flying braid. She could be scalped.

Time turned into a bellows, first puffing up to stretch out endlessly, then shrinking down flat into nothing. The day's final bells rang and Binnie shot out of the factory like a scalded cat. At home Mrs Howe studied Binnie's face closely and asked anxiously, "It went all right, I trust?"

Binnie understood her to mean quite a different question. What Mama really wanted to know was: Had Binnie done anything monumentally wrong or disgraced the name of Howe in some way? Binnie was still too stunned by the noise, bustle and surprises of the day to say much. She simply nodded. The silent nod satisfied Mrs. Howe and she jerked her head toward the dining room.

"Take the flapjacks in and then you sit down at the table there. No snatching at things, do you hear me? I want you to have a meal, sitting down like a body should."

A little uneasily, Binnie took a place at the end of the table nearest the kitchen. Never before had she sat down with the women. She felt peculiar, like an actress playing a part. Any moment she expected someone to point a finger at her and say, "You fraud. You don't belong here. Go back to being a little girl in the kitchen."

Still, getting first crack at the full platters passing by was an advantage, and she helped herself to a good stack of flapjacks.

"Hey, Mrs. Howe, make the corporation pay you double board money for Binnie," said Dorcas with her coarse gravel laugh. "She's eating more than two of us combined."

"She's got two needs, mind you. She has used her energy working a full day and she is still a young girl who needs nourishment to grow," Grace Little defended Binnie's appetite.

Good thing nobody measured how much she had actually done on this first day. Binnie thought guiltily that the boxes of bobbins she had carried that afternoon were too few to merit a day's pay.

The second day, Binnie was braced for the noise and only blinked a little when the machines started up.

"Your frames are stopped to doff."

Binnie's ears, more accustomed to the clatter now, could hear the warning cry when it came. Unload and load. The faster the filled bobbins were removed, the more yarn could be spun. The more yarn that was spun, the more cloth could be woven on the upper floors. Time was money and the doffers saved both for the mill.

The work was neither hard nor complicated but it was tiresome. Binnie made the long days pass more quickly by setting up challenges for herself. She aimed at beating her own speed, and like a glutton, she stuffed herself with new records of faster and faster time. By the end of the week she was carrying more bobbins than any other doffer. She wrote the number down in her birthday journal with great satisfaction and self-importance. She did not even mind her aching legs and tired feet. They were a badge proving that she belonged to the special sisterhood of working women.

Binnie loved the feeling of belonging. At night she lingered now at the table, relishing the last cup of tea and gossip. She herself talked with smug pride about "my throstles" and nodded knowingly when someone complained about the quality of the last cotton shipment.

Maria, who went to German lessons twice a week, was the first to leave the table. Her going reminded Binnie that she had still to deliver Mr. Pratt's supper, but she was enjoying herself too much to get up just then. When the evening traders knocked at the door, the easy air in the room turned brisk. These peddlers came every week to the door hawking goods and trinkets from candies to combs.

As Binnie was leaving, Florilla called to her, "Want to stroll after your chore? I'll join you. Their racket makes my head ache." She nodded toward the men who were joshing and bargaining loudly with Dorcas. "I need some fresh air."

Binnie left the supper pail with Mr. Pratt, then she and Florilla walked in agreeable silence away from the Print Works and the factories. After the hubbub of the mill and the clacking of the women, the hush of the evening gave Binnie the same relief as slipping into a cool stream on a hot day. The canals, dark green in the daytime, had turned a deep purple in the dusk. They lay smooth and still with a sleepy look to them. Seeing them now, you would never think those flat purple ribbons could be either powerful or dangerous. The sliding sound of slow-moving water was punctuated by the vigorous bass of a frog hidden in the darkening night.

Florilla's sudden exclamation told Binnie that she had smelled the smoke, too. They both turned quickly up the path forking to the left. Scrambling fast, Binnie could just keep up with Florilla's long steps. Why would the heavy smoke come through the pines in such curiously regular puffs, Binnie wondered.

Whew. Binnie let out her breath in relief. There was no burning house. The fire lay in two smudge pots under the fruit trees at the side of Granny Anna's. Frenchy was pulling a wet burlap across the tops of the pots, first one, then the other. Granny's voice rose shrill and bad tempered.

"Don't tell me, you no-account."

"No go! No go!" Frenchy's excited voice argued.

Spotting the newcomers, Granny shrieked to them. "Save me from this crazy Canuck. I'm never going to get any fruit. No, not one pippin nor one pear from these trees. They're infested so bad this year, I don't know what to do and that lazy man don't want to keep these fires going. How else, I ask you, are we going to chase out those bugs and worms or whatever they are?"

Frenchy stood his ground. Dropping the burlap, he closed his fists and turned his thumbs down to the ground, repeating loudly, "No go. They no go from zis."

It was true. A host of midges, mosquitoes and moths fluttered and flew beyond the fires but nothing came out of the trees.

"Soot. You need to soot them. Just plain smoke won't do it!" Florilla explained. "You want quick lime. You have to mix it two to one and then keep the whole windward."

Frenchy did not understand all the words but, recognizing the support, he flashed a brilliant smile at Florilla.

She raised her voice to the shout that she used with him

and repeated slowly, "Lime, quick lime. Make . . . use . . . *sooot*. Like chimney soot. And water, of course. You sprinkle the mix with water," she added in an afterthought.

"You know so much, you tell him," Granny said grudgingly. "Better, you show him and I'll give you all the sassafras tea you want."

Agreement at last. Frenchy breathed deeply with satisfaction.

"You come cook 'im with me. We cook togethair ze soot and all. You know good farming, eh, lady?" Frenchy said it admiringly.

Binnie could see the color rising in Florilla's cheeks even in the firelight. Nevertheless, Florilla, looking straight over the top of Frenchy's head, answered him firmly.

"Yes, I do. I'll come Sunday. You get the lime." Suddenly, she threw her arms up and with her horse laugh added, "*Poo-oof! Poof.* We'll make a big gas. All bugs go away then."

On the way home, Binnie blew her bottom lip out making an explosive *poo-oof* at the end. Florilla giggled at the sound. Every time Florilla managed to stop giggling, Binnie did it again. It seemed as if they laughed all the way. But at the door, Florilla sobered.

"Don't tell in the house, Binnie. You know how that Phoebe Little will talk. I shouldn't be doing work like that on the Sabbath, but that old lady and the Frenchy surely need help and that's the only time I have for it. Oh, don't you wish the days were longer yet?"

Binnie agreed. The pity was that you couldn't subtract some hours from dreary, too-long days and add them to those where you needed more time. Better yet, there ought to be a law that gave people the right to one whole day all to themselves, a totally free day with no Obligations of any kind.

Mama, too, was concerned about time that night. She scolded Binnie for not using her free time better.

"You know your stockings last year were getting too snug. If you don't start knitting soon, you will be sorry this winter," Mrs. Howe warned. "I don't have time to make any new stockings for you, Binnie. You must help yourself."

Binnie recognized the justice of Mama's remarks but disliked the idea of using her free time to sit and knit. Why, she hadn't had time enough yet to find Packy and tell him about working. And she had read hardly a page all week. The only free moments she had these days were between runs with the bobbins. Sometimes then she had as much as half an hour to wait before the next change. Sitting idly on the window sill, Binnie had wished that she could read, but there was no hope of that. Quimby's orders were to take away any books that the women carried in to work. Not even the Bible was excused from the rule of no books and no reading.

No, she couldn't read during the mill hours, but what if she took her knitting in? She hardly needed to look or use her eyes except for turning the heels. If she kept her attention fixed on the frames, surely there would be no cause for complaint?

She was right. None of the bosses objected when she carried in a newly started stocking the next morning. In fact, right after the noon bells, Susan, the younger doffer, brought in a piece of crewel work. She was cross-stitching a grinning lamb on a green field. Hannah, the lanky older girl who coughed a lot, leaned against the wall and watched them. A short woman with a wrinkled pudding face and round raisin eyes stopped and smiled approvingly.

"May all the saints have charge of you, me dears. If I wasn't kilt all over—especially me hands—with rheumatism, I'd be knitting, too."

Her rolling brogue made music out of the words. She was the Irish sweeper who cleaned up around the machines, one of the few Paddies working in the mills. Binnie didn't know her name or how to address her properly so she just asked the question abruptly.

"Do you know my friend, Packy McCabe? His mother is the widow McCabe and used to live in the Acre."

"Ach. How do I know that one? Childer is what we have most of in the Acre. Not much money but childer aplenty and more widows than Mercy should make. To know or pick out just one . . . ." The woman shook her head and walked on. Binnie was disappointed. She had hoped that the woman might know and tell Packy about her working in the mill. Susan was talking and Binnie brought her attention back to the girl at her side.

"I asked that one last week why she wore that red cloak in the summer. Do you know what she said?" In a crude imitation of the brogue, Susan squeaked, "Shur-rre, and if it plase Heaven, to kape cool." The girl laughed loudly at her own performance. "Plase Heaven," she repeated and laughed again.

Binnie stared at Susan. What was so funny about somebody saying words differently? Stupid laughter. If you thought about it, the woman made sense. Certainly, a loose cloak shielded one from the hot sun. Stupid girl.

The girl's laughter made Binnie feel as bristly as a hedgehog. She turned her back on the doffer and looked out the window. Binnie had a sudden longing to talk with a *real* friend. Tonight she would not linger at the table; she would go look for Packy.

Although Binnie had made up her mind, she went later than she had planned. She had to wait for Mama to finish a letter to Cousin Cornelia. Mrs. Howe was writing—though reluctantly—her permission for Aleck to stay longer. She gave it to Binnie with a reminder to look at the list in the Post Office.

"Adam should have gotten off a letter to us by now. You're not to pay more than twelve cents for it and if there isn't one, bring back my coppers. Don't drop them somewhere on the way."

Binnie left, muttering. She resented her mother's words. It was unsettling to be treated one minute like a hard-working woman, and the next like a careless child.

The usual large crowd had collected at the door of the Post Office. The women, hungry for mail from home, were ruthless in elbowing their way into the narrow passageway. Being short and skinny was a good thing, Binnie decided as she squeezed her way into spaces too small for anyone else. She stood on tiptoe to read the list of people who had letters waiting for them. Nothing for Howe. She butted and wiggled her way back to the street.

The lit store windows glowed like rich jewels, beckoning and tempting one inside. Binnie put the enticing stores behind her as she turned the corner by Wyman's Exchange. On this street which led to Packy's house, there were too few lights to compete with the last flush of pink from a late sunset. Binnie came to the top of the rise and saw a figure at the crossroads below. She knew instantly by the shape that it was Packy. In the dim light, he looked more square than ever, his spindly shanks like broom straws.

Binnie wished once again that she could whistle with two fingers in her mouth, but she had never mastered the knack. She cupped her hands around her mouth instead, and sent out a shrill cry.

"*Coo-ieee. Coo-ieee.*"

There. She had his attention now, for he had looked back over his shoulder. She ran swiftly down the slope to join him. He had not waited for her but he was walking slowly. Just as she reached him, he moved the large clothes basket that he was carrying up onto his right shoulder. He greeted Binnie abruptly after she fell into step with him.

"I just finished working. I got me a job. Not that," he said, tapping fingers against the basket. "That's my ma's. She's doing all the washing, the linens for the Washington Hotel."

How marvelous that he, too, should be working. Yet Binnie caught an odd note in his voice that puzzled her. She said simply, "Great. Great. Where you working?"

"Ha. Where else but where all good Paddies work? Diggin' in the dirt. Actually, I don't even do that. I'm the one who fills up the good ole Irish buggy."

Binnie could not see any part of his face. With no expression to clue her, she could not decide if he was joking or using a sour sarcasm. Dropping back a couple of paces, she changed sides, catching up again on the left.

After a long pause, she asked, "What's that? I mean what do you fill it with?" She felt somehow very young and ignorant.

"Stones. The rocks that the men break up with the pickax. I fill up the wheelbarrows."

She should have known. His face was tanned but streaked with road dust. His fingernails were broken and grimed. Binnie squinted to see better in the deepening dusk. His hunched shoulders and the loaded basket made him look deformed. Like some imp of Satan, she thought.

Binnie told him her own news in the fewest possible words. "I did it. I'm a doffer at the Merrimack Corporation."

"Wel-ll, so you've become one of the chosen people, huh? Did you change your bedtime prayers yet? Gotta give thanks, you know, to Kirk Boott, the Lord and Master Almighty, for his being so kind as to allow you to work for him."

There was no mistake: Packy was mocking her. Although she felt miserable, she could not resist trying again to spark some other feeling from him.

"Already I can carry more bobbins and faster than anybody," she offered.

"That's the way, Miss Goody. You knock yourself right out for them bigwig merchants in Boston. But you better keep your mind filled with honest thoughts and walk straight. Or they'll fire you quicker than a lightning bug can wink. Not even your good Yankee name will save you."

Binnie could hardly believe he had said it. What kind of talk was this from a friend? What had happened to the bond? The instant understanding? The ready sympathy?

"Leastways, I'm making money. I'll have earned almost ten dollars by this month's work," she argued.

"Yeah. But you know that money belongs by rights to

116

some man, some man who had maybe got a family to feed. And you took it away."

"What are you talking about? How could I be taking it away from some man? There's nothing but women working there and you know it. Except for overseers and *they* make twice or more what any of us girls can! How can you say what you just did?"

Binnie wondered how the conversation had taken this lunatic turn. She watched his mouth working and realized that he had a quid of tobacco in his mouth. If he didn't watch out, those nice sharp white teeth of his were going to turn all yellow and dirty with tobacco stains. She took a spiteful pleasure in the thought. He shifted the quid to one side with his tongue and spoke again.

"That's just what I mean. There's nothing but women in the mills because they're willing to work for 'most any kind of wage. If the corporations had to pay equal wages, if the law made them pay the same to women and same to men, why it stands to reason they'd hire more men. So long as they can get people like you—willing to work for practically nothing—they'll never hire a man."

They had reached the corner of his house. He put down the clothes basket and faced her. The moonlight washed the blue color out of his eyes and polished the whites to a glistening shine.

Binnie stared at him. She felt like a runner in a race where the rules kept changing. Any minute now this boy would tell her the goal was no longer "Get-as-much-money-as-fast-as-you-can." She was furious with Packy McCabe.

"Are you trying to tell me . . .? You can't mean that. Do you mean to say that I'm doing wrong just by working?"

"Uh-huh. Use your head . . . if you can." He paused to spit some tobacco juice out of the side of his mouth. "I'm not saying that *work* is bad. What I'm talking about is *where* you're working at and *who* you're working for. And"—his voice swelled with scornful pity—"those bosses have got you there for keeps because you don't learn nothing there that's any blessed use to you for any other work."

Binnie stuck her pointed chin out at him and answered fiercely, "You're wrong, Mr. Know-it-all. You're wrong. I'm learning lots and lots. Every day. Something new and valuable every day."

She crossed her fingers secretly to wipe out the lie and vowed to herself that she would find a way to make it true.

"Ha!" he snorted. "When you get tired of being a servant to an army of machines, you come and I'll talk to you again, little Bin-kins."

"When pigs fly, I will," Binnie shouted. Tears of pure rage promised to spill over in a minute. "When pigs fly, that's when I'll come looking for you again, you rotten jealous boy!"

She turned and ran away. The straggling cowpath road was filled with unexpected dips and stones. She got up the hill in a short-lived burst of speed, stumbling and tumbling. Once out of his sight, she slowed to a trot but whipped her rage up again. She must have a head softer than stewed pumpkin to think that he was a friend. Never again. She would never make that mistake again.

As she lay in bed that night, Binnie worked out how she would make him sorry. First, she would go into every part of the factory and learn everything that went on and how every machine worked. She would know so much and be so necessary to them, they would ask her to oversee the whole works. She guessed that maybe that part would take about ten years to accomplish.

Then one day *he* would come begging for work and she would look right through him and say they weren't hiring just then.

From far off in the hills, the musical wailing of a whippoorwill floated into the night air. She felt a strong kinship with the sad-sounding bird. Binnie had never laid eyes on a whippoorwill yet. Nor was she likely to see one. These days she was too tied up to go jaunting. She wondered who might have seen one up close. Maybe Packy would . . . . Binnie jerked her mind away from that track.

"I hate his gizzard and guts," she whispered to herself in the dark. "I'll walk to China on my knees before I ever talk to him again."

A new thought struck Binnie. For such a vow to be truly satisfying, Packy McCabe should know about it. How could she make him aware of it if she never spoke to him again? Binnie brooded over the problem without finding an answer. Short of telling him straight out, she could not find a way to get around the "never" part of her vow.

"Daresay I shall think of a way," she told herself and fell asleep.

ᏋᎧ10

Binnie had no trouble keeping her oath in the days that followed. Going from house to mill and back again to the house, four trips a day every day but Sunday, Binnie never saw Packy McCabe. But she could not forget his angry, pricking words. They popped into her mind often and wiggled there like live worms.

He was right, she admitted to herself. After the first day at work, there had been nothing to learn and the boring back-and-forth with the bobbin boxes developed no skills. Binnie no longer cared how many she carried in a day and the long days seemed longer and more tiresome still. She longed for the Fourth of July when the mills would be closed. Binnie knew exactly what she wanted to do on the holiday. She would feast on all the sights, sounds and smells that she had been longing for and missing because she had to work.

First, she wanted the smell of a farmer's fresh-cut hay curing in the sun. If she couldn't get enough of the smell by walking through a meadow, she would stop and push her nose smack up against a haystack.

Then she planned to stand very, very still deep in the silence of the woods to hear the liquid, gurgling songs of the veery and the wood thrush.

Out in the sunshine again, she would hunt for spiders' webs by the falling-down timbers of the old footbridge. With luck, she might find one with a perfect dewdrop hanging in the lacy web. Or, with luck and the right timing, she might find one still being woven by the spider. She would lie there and watch for as long as she wanted. No boss would command her to hurry; no ringing bells would interrupt her.

Finally, she would scout out the town's celebrations planned in honor of Independence Day. The only defect to the day—and it was a tiny one—was that Aleck was not home to keep her company.

Dawn of the longed-for holiday saw Binnie sliding out of bed and moving quickly but quietly around the kitchen. She scraped all the leftovers from the larder into her bowl. Cold boiled potato, some soggy clumps of blueberry cobbler and the dried out gingerbread. She covered all of it with buttermilk and a heavy lashing of molasses. The sour-sweet mush sat like a stone at the bottom of her stomach. With a breakfast like that to hold her, she could even miss her dinner.

Binnie opened the back door to cipher out the weather. It was a muzzy, delicate day but the grayness looked like the kind that would burn off quickly. Bright blobs of color at her feet caught her eye. A neatly rounded bouquet of garden flowers sat on the doorstep. Binnie picked it up and sniffed with pleasure. Who could have . . . and when?

Cosmos, bachelor's buttons, one rose as big as a doorknob. The nosegay was framed by a collar of sweet fern and held together by a scrap of wet cheesecloth around the stems. Binnie grinned. Someone must have raided a richly flowering garden.

Had Frenchy with his extravagant manners left it in thanks for the meals and help Mama and Florilla gave him? Maybe Porky-Dorky with her simpering smiles had managed to sucker a peddler into a declaration? No matter. Binnie liked the smell and took the offering as a cheery omen. With such a happy beginning, the new day ahead was bound to be special. She put the flowers in a mug of water on the table and left.

The sun's full rays fell on her just as she reached Cave's Hill. On the back or short side was the shallow cave that children used for games of Pirates and Indians, but when she was alone Binnie preferred the long slope. Today the hill did not seem as steep as it once had.

Moved by her memories, Binnie picked up the bottom edge of her skirt and wound it just above her knees like a swaddling cloth. She tucked the end into her waistband. Lying down on the crest, she set herself in motion with a hard push. She rolled and rolled, picking up more and more speed. The dizzying descent was always spiced by the dangerous possibility of rolling into a tree or hard up against a rock. At the bottom, she lay safe, breathless and laughing.

The sky had barely stopped swinging overhead when she spied the figure moving boldly out of the thicket just beyond where she lay. Binnie stopped laughing. Packy McCabe was making straight for her. Only a few feet separated them. A shudder of anger swept Binnie to her feet. She stuck her tongue out at him and started away. There was no hope, really, for she was heading uphill and he was a faster runner than she. Packy finished the chase in one swift move. He made a flying tackle that caught her just at the bend of the knees. Binnie fell up against the hill with a thump.

"Sit down so I can explain," he roared, ducking and dodging her kicking feet. He anchored her feet easily by sitting on them. "You have to listen and understand."

"I don't *have to* anything. I don't have to do anything you say and you can't make me, mister," Binnie yelled back at him even louder.

"You *will so*. You'll let me tell it out of the face." One look at Binnie's blank face and he explained: "Tell it from beginning to end. No interruption. No din, Bin." His grin was hesitant, the bright blue eyes begging her to smile at his weak rhyme.

Binnie glared at him in mute rage and twisted her body, turning as far away from him as she could. But Packy McCabe ignored her message.

"I been eating chagrin since I saw you. What I said wasn't meant for you to tease yourself about. It wasn't meant about *you*. It was the *system* I was talking about, the system. Did you know my uncle has experience working on the big spinning machines, the ones they call 'mules', down Rhode Island? And do you know what they said to him over to the Appleton Corporation? 'We got throstles and we don't need no experienced mule spinners. The girls manage the throstles and cost us lots less than any mule men.' And after they heard him talking they said they didn't need anybody at all, not in spinning, no, and not even in the carding nor in the picking."

His mind boggled on the last thought, for he repeated it in stunned disbelief: "Not even in the picker house. Why any ignoramus, any fool, can do that dirty work and it's no wonder they don't pay hardly at all for it. No work, no jobs . . . leastways not for Irishers.

"My uncle says wait, just wait. Because all the mills—Appleton included, they're all going to have to go to mule spinning soon. Why, even now throstles ain't good enough; they can't make nothing but that coarse stuff: the sheetings and jean cloth, and some calicoes. If they don't put in new machines, they can't compete. It takes strength, a man's strength, to run those big mules, but you get a finer, stronger thread off a mule."

He fell silent just as Binnie took a quick look from the corner of her eye. He sat still and brooding. When he spoke again, his voice had dropped to a soft, bitter whisper.

"Meanwhile, we gotta eat, so both of us are digging those buggy, stinking holes for the new canals and the road. Damn Yankees. For that kind of work, they don't mind how we talk. You know what it's like to sweat and work and have people walk past and talk about you like you wasn't there? Like you was a dog? They laugh about how we talk, about where we come from, about how we act and pray. We're not the animals. They are! Pigs! But I wasn't blaming you, Binnie. It's just that some of those damn Yankees had made me so mad that very day."

The words had rushed out in one full flood. Now he spoke more slowly.

"Only thing, Binnie, what I said to you about their firing you? You know that's true. For all they paint up the boarding houses so pretty every year and take care that everybody should go to church, the corporations don't really care about you. You know that, don't you, Binnie?"

He paused, waiting, but still she said nothing.

"It seems to me a friend, a *real* friend, could say *that* to a friend and not have it held against him? Don't you think?"

All the while he spoke, Binnie had been both thinking and remembering. She had been thinking of the anger, the pride, the hurt, the caring—all the great welter of feelings exposed by the storm of his words. She remembered her very first meeting with him and her vow never, never to speak to him again.

Never, she decided, was a piece of time impossible to measure; it had no beginning and no ending to it and so, no meaning. Besides, it was her turn to be generous in understanding.

"Mm-mmm," she said. "Push off, Packy. You're too fat for my feet, Packy."

The use of his name was on purpose, a signal that they were friends again. He slid off her feet and sat with knees humped up under his chin. Binnie, who was snapping off dandelion heads with her thumb, was visited by a sudden hunch.

She said, "I love summer, don't you? I love summer because of all the flowers."

She darted a quick look at him. Under his tan, Packy McCabe had reddened to a deep rusty red. He stared straight ahead, avoiding her eyes.

"Yeah. My ma does, too. She's—uh—crazy for flowers," he muttered.

He jumped up and, still looking ahead at the thicket, he said in a suddenly too-loud voice, "Hey, that was a nifty idea you had. Let's go again."

Binnie watched the red-faced Packy running up the hill. She was positive that she had guessed right. At the top, Packy tucked his hands into his armpits. He flapped his folded arms like wings and crowed, "*Cockadoodledeedo.*"

"Look out below." He bellowed his warning and threw himself down the hill in a fast, reckless roll.

What a looney he is, Binnie thought with delight and

charged up the hill to follow suit. They rolled again and again until they had beaten down the grass in a wide swath and their tongues hung dry and panting. They rolled until they were streaked with grass stains and smelled of dew-wet earth. Finally, one yelled "quits" and they sprawled, resting at the bottom.

Then Binnie began to talk. For days her eyes and ears had been doing duty for her tongue: watching, listening, but saying nothing. Now she had someone who was willing to listen to her. No, better than that: someone who was curious and interested in what she had to say.

She told Packy how every conversation in the mill looked like plotting because only heads bent close together could hear one another in that overwhelming noise. She described how thick the air was with gray lint fuzzballs. How these fuzzballs landed on everyone's head, turning even young women into hoary old ones. She told him how two women had fainted yesterday in the close, stuffy air of the dressing room. How fainting became a common occurrence in the spinning room in the summer because all the windows were nailed shut.

Packy, startled, interrupted her. "Why do that? Windows are for people to breathe. Why nail them shut?"

"It's to keep their precious old threads from drying out and snapping. That's more important than any woman as far as the bosses are concerned. The workers are supposed to keep on going no matter what. Just like the machines." Binnie made a face that showed what she thought of that sentiment.

She declared—and what a relief it was to say it out loud —her dislike for pious Mr. Quimby. She reported his insulting question to her when she stepped up to sign for her pay: "Can you write your own name then, girl?"

Packy's blue eyes glinted with amusement but he sympathized with her feelings. A loud crash from the direction of town distracted Binnie and sent her scrambling to her feet.

"The cannons!" she exclaimed. "I forgot the celebrations. And I was supposed to march to Chapel Hill grove with the Sabbath School. Oh, dear, if they're shooting off the salutes, it must be noon already."

Binnie was brushing herself off, trying to erase or at least blur the grass stains.

"Come with me, Packy. After the orations, there'll be tables and tables of good things to eat. The 'piscopalians always have more lemonade than anybody. I'll just pretend that I was stuck at the back of the procession."

"Join you? So all those ladies can look at the 'quare critter' that I am? No, no thanks," he said.

Binnie fumed to herself: of all the times for him to get in a pucker. This holiday was too short to waste. Binnie wanted his company for the rest of the day, so she chose her next words carefully.

"You're judging beforehand and that's unfair. How do you know what different people will do? You're unfair and lily-livered, too. Aren't you the one who had a granfa'r fight in the Revolution? How can anybody be mindful that the holiday is *your* birthright, too, if you don't even show up at the Independence celebrations? Besides, we'll go by my house and I can give you the book. Remember? Patrick Henry?"

Binnie thought that the great orator, Patrick Henry himself, could not have put together a better mix of challenge, appeal and temptation. But she was afraid that one more word would be peppering the pot with too heavy a hand so she turned away and started walking toward town.

"Will you listen to the chee-ild? She's a ninny talking sweet nonsense. And just who do you think is going to check up on whether Packy McCabe shows himself at the festivities? Why, in that crowd an elephant could be dancing on the table and nobody would notice."

Binnie marveled at how the contrary boy could back up on his own words. First he was positive that people were going to single him out; then he was convinced that not even God would notice his presence. But she felt certain now that he would join her and she was right.

"But I'm that fond of lemonade and I'd enjoy doing some of those Protestants out of their share . . . so I'll go along with you." Packy fell into step beside her and she had to bite the inside of her cheek to keep from grinning.

To get their lemonade they had to pay a price. Everyone in the grove on Chapel Hill had to sit first through two long hours of passionate speeches about the struggle for liberty and the need to preserve it. Packy listened with alert and amused interest but Binnie almost fell asleep.

Fortunately, there was enough lemonade to make the wait worthwhile. Packy watched with increasing respect as Binnie put away almost a half gallon without stopping. With their stomachs gorged, they lay in the shade of the trees talking about the story sweeping through the crowd.

Shocked voices swore that Kirk Boott had raised the English flag on the same pole but *above* the American flag. Unforgivable, said some; untrue, said others. The debate raised the pitch of voices to a higher and livelier hum.

"Small difference whether it's true," Packy argued. "That man's got no love for democracy or plain people. He's so high and mighty that even if he didn't do it, he would have done it if he'd thought about it."

"I'd sooner have a bee make his home in my ear than buy your kind of talk with all those 'ifs,'" Binnie said, shaking her head. "Hey, boy, let's get out of here," she urged suddenly and tugged Packy to his feet. A robust young woman with a rolled-up paper and a determined expression was heading in their direction.

"C'mon. That woman is one of the Temperance ladies and she's looking for people to sign up in the Cold Water Army. You'll be reading and reciting the pledge before you know it."

"What are you worried about? You got ambitions, or plans maybe, to becoming a drunkard?" Packy asked with a mocking smile, but he moved swiftly as he spoke.

After they got away, Packy said, "Speaking of pledges reminds me. What about that book you promised?"

On the way to pick up the book, they detoured to look at Boott's house. There were no flags of any kind to be seen, so that debate ended on the spot. They deposited the book at Packy's house and then circled back to the center of town where the narrow streets were jammed with people, carriages and horses.

Packy nudged Binnie to look at the group of Penobscots who stood with solemn stillness on the corner. The Indians must have tied up their boats at the old campground on Musquash Island. She could not tell the men from the women since they all dressed exactly alike. They wore a curious mix of American and Indian garments: tall stovepipe hats, loose baggy cotton gowns over hide leggings and moccasins.

Mill women still in Sabbath finery eddied and swirled in the streets as they visited with friends. It looked as if every one of Lowell's seventeen thousand citizens had come to occupy the same three blocks. A good many must have toasted the holiday with large quantities of beer and hard cider, for the whole crowd verged on being rowdy.

Binnie darted out, calling "City Hall" over her shoulder to Packy. He nodded understanding and caught up with her as she fell in behind a farmer's wagon. Following in the wake of the wagon was easier than clearing their own way.

Tickets to the concert at City Hall cost twenty-five cents but on such a warm evening the windows would be wide open; those outside would hear almost as well as those in the hall. Binnie was too occupied choosing a good spot under the window to see the tall man careening toward her. He narrowly missed crashing into her, his elbow grazing her ear.

"Brats! Snot-nosed brats!" he said as he stumbled off the edge of the boardwalk.

He stood there swaying like a wind-tossed tree. Packy, who had grabbed her arm to pull her out of the way, looked at the man with loathing.

"You see that one? He's from England. You stay away from him. He's different."

"Well, I *know* that." She had heard clearly his accent. "So what?" Binnie's brows had arched with surprise. She had not expected Packy of all people to have a quarrel with someone for being "different."

"Next week is Boyne," said Packy.

"What's that? And what's it got to do with the price of

tea?" Binnie was exasperated with Packy, whose explanations were not explaining anything.

"I forget you're not one of us," Packy said with a sigh. "Back in the Old Country, there's this river, the Boyne. It starts by Trinity Well which has holy waters." He saw a fascinated disbelief in Binnie's eyes and hurried on.

"Anyway, that's not the important part. The thing is, some couple hundred years since, there was a big battle by the river. See, the Irish had their troubles with the English kind of like the Americans did. But some Irish—what they call 'Orangemen'—joined the English and old King Billy to beat down the other Irishmen who wanted to be independent."

He amended himself. "*Catholic* and independent. The Croppies, the Catholics, fought against the Orangemen and they lost in this Battle of the Boyne."

"But what's that old battle to do with this drunken man?"

"Boggs—that's his name, he's overseer at the Dye House —that Boggs doesn't think the Croppies got beat up enough. Last year on the Anniversary, he came through the Acre swinging a shillelagh, looking for Croppies to bash in the head."

Binnie's eyes had opened wide at Packy's last words. "And what did they . . . what do they do back?"

"Fight. To tell the truth, the Croppies are still fighting that old battle all over again, too. It gets pretty bloody sometimes."

"What a waste . . . trying to get even with somebody for something done two or three hunderd years ago. I can't believe all you people." She shook her head in amazement.

"My ma says that The History has gotten bred into the

bones and carried by the blood in every Irishman so they can't help themselves now. They *have* to fight one another." Packy sounded apologetic. Then his voice grew firm and positive. "But I tell you that Boggs is different and I mean just that. He *likes* the blood and broken bones. You ever smell rum on him, get out of his way. Rum lights him up so he goes roaring just like a fire through dry woods and he's just as hurtful, too."

Binnie shivered as she looked at the man who stood swaying on the corner. Now that she knew about him, every feature in the face took on an evil cast. The round black peppercorn eyes looked hard and mean; the mouth looked like he sucked vinegar.

"That man lives over by you," Packy warned. "He's in John Bull's Row, those brick cottages, with all the other print and dye workers from England. Don't you forget what I said about him."

Binnie nodded. "I won't forget." She appreciated Packy's concern but she wanted to change the subject. She did not want his gloomy words to color the end of her holiday. "Listen, listen to the music."

The two violins which had been tuning up were singing the opening bars of "Nid Noddin." A Kent Bugle cut in to carry the tune soaringly out over the street sounds and Binnie sighed with pleasure. The concert ended with a loud chorus of "Sweet's the Hour When Freed from Labor" to which Binnie added "Yea, amen!" in loud agreement.

At the end of the concert, neither Binnie nor Packy discussed when or where they would meet again. It went without saying they would find each other to talk. Walking home, Binnie remembered how timid and suspicious she had been at their first meeting. She figured that Packy McCabe was the first friend she had made by choice rather than by circumstance. Weezy Whipple had become a friend because they shared the same desk at school, while Florilla and Maria just happened to live in the same house with her. Whereas Packy McCabe, who lived in a world quite removed from hers, was that rarest and best kind of friend, one who shared her view of the world. And when he saw things differently, he allowed she had the right to disagree.

Binnie walked slowly. She felt big with contentment. Mama was sure to be annoyed with her for staying away from the house all day but Binnie didn't care. This perfect day was worth whatever scolding she would collect tonight.

11

Binnie had braced herself to meet her mother but was unprepared for the crowded jumble of tense people she found in the kitchen: Dorcas hunched over a mug of herbal tea, Maria perched on the very edge of a straight chair and an erect Florilla clutching the back of another with a grip that turned her knuckles white. Mrs. Howe sat in the oak rocker, pumping it in short jerky bursts, a sure sign of upset.

Ignoring Binnie's arrival, Mrs. Howe addressed Florilla. "Do you mean to say you told him how much money you have in the bank?"

"Yes, I did. He asked if I was a saver-y woman," Florilla

answered. She had a defiant edge to her voice, like a naughty child caught out.

"But don't you see that might have given him . . ."—Maria hesitated—"that . . . might have given him ideas?" She finished her sentence in a delicately questioning tone.

"NO!" Florilla almost shouted her answer. "He asked me to go away with him *first*. Before he asked about money, he asked me to be his . . . his . . . *femme*."

The word was foreign but the meaning was crystal clear even to Binnie. Her mouth dropped open as she heard it. Florilla's long jaw jutted out further than usual. She spelled out her intentions.

"He asked me to go away with him and I tell you that I *am* going. Tonight . . . now. Frenchy will be by here any minute to get me."

Binnie, who had been mulling over the pleasures of her friendships all the way home, was shaken by the thought of losing Florilla. She started to cry out "Don't go," but the babble of voices was too loud and confusing for her to be heard.

"Do you know what going without two weeks' notice to the boss means?" Maria asked. "Do you realize that the corporation will put you on the blacklist?"

Binnie's mind had hop-skipped to another question. She interrupted to ask, "How much do *they* give?"

Mrs. Howe looked at Binnie for the first time. "Who gives what? What are you talking about?" she asked, bewildered.

"How much notice does the corporation give when they lay off workers?" Binnie said.

"The corporation is not obliged to give workers any notice. What foolishness are you talking?"

"No matter," said Dorcas in a tired voice. She was obviously feeling sick again. Every month or two, it seemed, Dorcas got whey-faced with stomach cramps. She swallowed some tea and added, "She'd be on the blacklist even if she had time to give notice. She hasn't completed a year with the corporation the way she signed for. Remember?"

"If something happens, you'll have no way to get a living for yourself," said Mrs. Howe. "Once you're on that blacklist, no corporation anywhere will hire you. You do know, Florilla, that they send that list down Rhode Island way, New Hampshire, even clear to Pennsylvania. Without your honorable discharge papers from the Merrimack, you'll not be able to come back here, either." Her voice was stern in warning.

"I don't care. I don't care," said Florilla.

Maria tried again. "Florilla, as your friends . . . no, more than that. We stand in place of family to you. We ask you . . . have you weighed . . . ? Is it worth giving up your living, your friends, your church, maybe . . . for this man?"

Maria sounded calm as always, but her hands gave her away. They twisted anxiously, with the fingers twining, steepling and curling around each other.

Binnie thought there were more important questions to be asked. Like where was Florilla going and would she write to them after she got there.

Florilla's speech raced like a runaway locomotive. "What do you want me to do? Spend thirty, forty more years in the factory nursemaiding those machines? Hoping year after year I can save enough to rent a room somewhere after I retire so's I can die? Or do you think my brother's so-loving wife will open her arms to take me back into *her* house?" She paused and then said in a harsh, demanding voice, "Look at me. Just look at me. I'm close to thirty now. Who else do you think is going to ask a horse like me to marry him?"

Maria broke in. "But that's another thing. Are you going to marry him? Is he Catholic or what? Where are you going to find a minister at this hour?"

"We're stopping on the way to Buffalo." Florilla sounded less certain now.

Dorcas gave a raspberry sound of disbelief and the sound spurred Florilla.

"You want to know the truth, the *real* truth? I don't care if we stop or not. I'm going and nothing you all say can stop me. It's my first and only chance to make my life happy and I'm willing to gamble that it's a good chance."

Florilla had let go of the chair finally. Now she moved forward to sit in it. Her voice grew softer, begging them to understand.

"All those people moving out West . . . well, they have to go through Buffalo first. He's got a friend, a wheelwright out there who's got so much work, who needs help so bad he'll pay the moon and the stars for a good carpenter. Frenchy can do the carpentering. And land is dog-cheap there. He promised me that with my money we can buy a little piece where I can do the farming."

"He is a good carpenter, I'll say that," Mrs. Howe admitted. "And a good cook," she added unexpectedly.

Binnie had been much struck by the earlier picture that Florilla had painted of her future. Now she decided that the pairing of Florilla and Frenchy made a crazy kind of sense. She could see Florilla working happily in her hayfield and vegetable garden while Frenchy cheerfully—no, proudly—cooked the meals for both of them.

Mrs. Howe broke the silence that had followed her last remark. "What arrangements are you going to make about the money? Once you've gone from Lowell, how do you expect to get it from the bank? Can he write . . . ." A knocking at the door interrupted her and she finished dryly, "Talking of the devil, he's come to speak for himself." She went to let him in.

Cap in hand, Frenchy swept them all a deep bow. He clapped the canvas cap back on his springy black curls and strutted over to Florilla's side. He was so sure of his welcome that he boldly put his arm around her waist.

" 'allo. She tell you, yes? She don' like mill better as me so I 'ave a *femme*," he said, beaming at the other women and Binnie.

The two standing side by side made a comical pair. Frenchy looked to Binnie like a small stunted alder being crowded down by a spreading oak. His head barely topped Florilla's shoulder. He tilted his head back and gave Florilla a look that was plainly one of admiration.

"I got me big, strong woman, no? She so big she make *très joli* babees, *très* big babees for me, yes?"

Mrs. Howe sat down abruptly in the rocker with a thump. She held a handkerchief up over her face and was making a peculiar noise. Binnie could not tell whether she was crying, sneezing or laughing. Florilla gave a small strangled sound and blushed. Binnie studied her with fascinated respect. She had not believed that anybody could produce a color so deep yet so bright.

Looking from Florilla to Frenchy and back again to Florilla, Binnie felt suddenly as if she had borrowed Frenchy's eyes. Once you accepted the large scale that Florilla was built on, if you thought that big meant better, then everything about her looked good.

The too-long jaw full of even white teeth spelled good health; the broad shoulders, the big hands and feet foretold mountains of hard work, while the well-muscled arms and ample curving bosom promised a cosy shelter for little ones.

Yes, there were daintier, prettier and younger women in Lowell, but Binnie could understand why Frenchy thought he had won a prize. When Florilla looked down at him with a goofy kind of grin, Binnie realized, too, that the feeling between them was mutual. It was Frenchy himself—curls, dimple and cheery manners—that she prized and wanted, not just any man.

"'ey, we go now. The wagon of ze farmer ees waiting. It go for Springfield tonight."

Frenchy's words sent the women scattering like buckshot: Florilla to collect her baggage, Mrs. Howe to make up a packet of food for the trip, Maria to find paper and sealing wax for the bank letters. Florilla took only a tied shawl-bundle with her. When the couple had a settled address, the money and trunk would be sent out to them.

Florilla dipped down on one knee to give Binnie a bone-squeezing hug and said in a choky voice, "Promise you'll keep growing but not too fast."

Rising, she spoke to Dorcas who still sat glumly drinking tea.

"Dorcas, I want you to have my oiled silk umbrella, the yellow one that I've left by my bed. I do appreciate no end what you did."

She looked down for a moment at herself and smoothed

138

the skirt of her dress. Then they were gone. Mama went slowly to latch the door behind them. Silence fell on the kitchen with almost the force of a hard slap. Binnie sighed so deeply that it just escaped being a sob.

"Sighs are a bad sauce for your supper, Binnie. And why are you so late for your supper?" said Mrs. Howe as she put a bowl on the table. "Get some bread and milk for your meal. Dorcas, has that tea made your cramps any better?"

"It will, I guess. In a while," Dorcas answered with a grimace. "Can you imagine living way out in some cow town? Anyway, where d'you suppose she got any money to tempt him with? She just moved up from being a spare hand last month. She hasn't hardly had time to earn money, much less lay up any sum in the bank."

"By rights, half that farm in Vermont should have been hers. Heaven knows she did more than half the work on it," said Mrs. Howe. "Her brother must have had a bad conscience because he gave her a small sum when the bride threw Florilla out."

Dorcas's eyebrows shot up. "You mean she had real money all her own? Why'd she bother with that Canuck foreigner? She should have sat tight and piled up some more. She could probably catch someone real worthwhile, not a sprat that can't even look her in the eye. And hardly able to talk with her besides."

Poor Porky-Dorky. She didn't want Frenchy herself or to live in the wilds of Buffalo. Still, it galled her to know that Florilla had been invited to marry while she herself lingered on, waiting. Dorcas Boomer was surely chewing sour grapes tonight, Binnie thought.

"But he's man enough for all purposes and he suited her," said Mrs. Howe.

Binnie could tell Mama was close to losing her patience and all sympathy for Dorcas. Dorcas must have felt it, too, for she dropped the subject and rose to collect the clean soft rags from the drying string in the corner.

"I'll tend to those that are soaking in the morning."

Dorcas had nodded toward the basin of cold water sitting on the three-legged stool. All the women used that same basin to soak rags; there was rarely a day in the month when it was empty. The rags, which were cut roughly to the same size, all looked alike to Binnie but each woman took care to wash and collect only her own.

Dorcas couldn't leave without a parting remark. "It's all the same to me whether those girls run away *with* a man or run away *from* one. It's really a blessing when they go. Thanks to that Harriet's going, I finally got enough pegs for my clothes. We all can use a little more room to ourselves."

Binnie thought that was scratching pretty hard to find a silver lining in tonight's cloud. For herself, she couldn't think of a single good side to Florilla Nappet's leaving.

Yet, within the week, Binnie found herself grateful for Florilla's empty bed. A fierce, scorching and seemingly endless heat spell settled on Lowell. Binnie took Florilla's bed by a window gladly, although the attic itself was unbearably hot. At least in that bed, she could toss and turn without bumping into Mama's sweating body. Binnie rose from baking in a hot bed at night to face an even hotter day at work.

The factory was like a furnace. Friction from the leather belts moving and the machine parts turning sent still more heat into air that was already too thick to breathe. The choking cotton dust and the tight-shut windows wiped out any possible cooling that the thick brick walls and high ceilings might have provided.

Between her doffing stints, Binnie wandered to other floors and other rooms looking for distraction and relief. She knew better than to go into the weaving rooms where hundreds of flying shuttles slammed into the carriages of the looms with a head-splitting bang. The racket in there made the spinning rooms seem like quiet, restful retreats.

Binnie climbed the stairs to the dressing room with dragging footsteps. She looked in at the women who were brushing on the sizing that stiffened the warp threads. They were working in a deadly silence. Hot size was less lumpy and easier to apply than cold size. But the heat necessary to keep it smooth-flowing sent more sweat pouring through the already soaked kerchiefs tied around their foreheads. No point to entering that room; it was the worst one of all.

Binnie thought briefly of going down to the cloth room where Maria Teasdale worked. It would be quiet in there for there were no machines, but Maria, who measured, folded and marked the finished cloth, liked working in silence and did not welcome company. Besides, Binnie decided, she might run into Quimby on the way. He had taken to smiling and patting her approvingly every time he saw her. She loathed being touched by him and tried to stay out of his way as much as possible.

Binnie turned reluctantly back to the spinning room. The whirling spindles had stopped. It was past time for her to carry new bobbins but she did not hurry. The heat had deadened her every desire except the one to escape.

Binnie could not decide which she hated most: the choking cotton dust, the thick, rancid smell of the oil and tallow used to grease the machines or the foul smells from the loosely boarded necessary on the first floor. She never used either that necessary or the privy out in the mill yard. She much preferred to make a quick dash to the outhouse at home where the air was more breathable.

Binnie carried the bobbin boxes to the frames at a slow walk. Even so, her armpits were clammy with sweat, her swollen feet throbbing by the time she came back to sit by the window. Though shut tight, it had plants on the sill, so there was a faint smell of earth and growing things.

A picture popped suddenly into her head. She saw a small ball tethered to a paddle. Little children loved the toy because the ball never rolled away.

That's what I am, she realized abruptly, recognizing why the picture had come into her head. A tethered ball. When she wandered too far, when she sat dreaming about something else, the tethering cry of "Doffers, we need doffers" always yanked her back.

After supper, she followed her usual practice and hunted up Packy. They went directly to the river where it was cooler. Packy balanced on a sharp peaked rock while she straddled two small flat ones at the side of the waterfalls. She told him about the picture in her head.

"You've got the right of it and a right fancy way with words as well," he said.

He leaned out into the spray to cool his face. He had reminded her of something else that she wanted to share.

"Listen," she said to his back. "I want to talk with you about right . . . or maybe I mean rights?"

She spoke slowly, her face shadowed by the worrying question in her mind.

"You know how we sign a contract or agreement to work? It says we have to give the corporation two weeks notice before we leave. Well, today Quimby fired Hannah on the spot. She had hiked her skirts up 'cause it's so hot and unbuttoned the top of her bodice. *He* said it was immoral conduct but I think he was looking to get rid of her. She has this bad cough and kept missing so many days. The spinners have to do their own doffing when anyone is out and he didn't like that."

"Mmm-mm."

Packy had jumped onto the hard bank and now sat down. Binnie followed him.

"You're not listening."

"I am. Go on, what's the rub? Bosses have always got the right to hire and fire."

"I want you to think some more about it. Like, think on what kind of rights do workers have? From what I hear, she won't get any money this month at all. Because it's not a full month of work, he's holding back the wages for the six or seven days she *did* work. She earned that money. Isn't that hers by rights?"

"Seems so to me," Packy said cautiously. "Did he decide on his own to dock her wages or is it written someplace in the agreement?"

"Written, I think." Binnie shrugged. "I don't know for sure. But why doesn't the contract spell out some of our rights? Like making the company give *us* notice before they cut off our work? And, another thing: Why do they get to keep money that's worked for? It's a lopsided agreement that gives all the rights to one side and puts only obligations and requirements on to the other side, to us factory girls."

"I agree." Packy was silent for a long time. He said finally, "It's a free country but you don't have much choice, do you? They've got you in a stranglehold. Unless you want to be a hired girl in somebody's house . . . or maybe teach school, there's hardly nothing for women. Nothing that pays hard cash. It's surely not right, but I just don't see how or what you can do about it."

"I think it's grossly unfair. Quimby is grossly unjust."

"Here I just decided that the damn Yankees in this town are not all bad and now you're trying to change my mind."

"What d'you mean?" a puzzled Binnie asked.

Packy had put a mock frown on his face. His heavy black eyebrows made a deep V that reminded Binnie of a blackbird's wing. His extra casual air masked a deep excitement.

"Just what I said. I've been waiting to tell you. This man who lives by us—Jim North—he works in the Machine Shop, see. He came by when I was working on the outside pump. My ma couldn't hardly get any water so I tinkered with it. Besides that, I fixed it to shut off itself slow and gradual-like. North, he spied what I was doing and asked if I was a mechanic. Then he said: maybe would I like to *be* a mechanic? He meant it, too. I'm to go around to the shop on Saturday. That's a slow day so the boss can look me over and see if I can read from the sketches and how well I can do arithmetic. I'd say it was a good chance for me." He finished coolly, but the three jabs in a row that he gave her on the arm betrayed his excitement.

Binnie was speechless for a moment. "Good chance" was

144

a mild way to describe it. All over America new mills and manufactories were being built; all of them needed machines, tools, parts and fittings. Those who learned the mechanician's skills could command the highest wages and never lack for work. The Lowell Machine Shop made everything from simple water pipes for big cities like Boston to locomotive engines for the new and spreading railroad lines. The prospect for Packy was a golden one, a chance almost too good to be dreamed about. Binnie hoped there was no envy in her voice when she spoke.

"I got a cousin working there. He's supposed to be a clever fellow. If you go in the shop, look for Elias Howe and tell him you know us Lowell Howes. Maybe he'll be a friend to you, too. Though he's older than you. Like sixteen, I think."

"That's *if*—you forget—that's *if* I become a 'prentice's helper. I wouldn't be surprised if he came around on his own to help a newcomer. You Howes make a habit of doing good turns for others."

"Turns is turn-about." Binnie spoke tartly but she was pleased. "We better turn ourselves around back into town. It's getting late and those stupid bells will be ringing too soon in the morning for my taste."

The dark evening sky had streaks of darker clouds running through it, looking like trails of dirt left by a careless broom. Binnie stooped and picked some leaves off a wintergreen plant whose scent had been teasing her nose. She passed a couple to Packy and chewed slowly on the two remaining. The cooling juicy taste reminded her of summers past when she had roamed freely every day.

They cut across the edge of a cranberry meadow and skirted a small corn field garnished with a scarecrow. Passing the bushy cornstalks, Binnie sighed. Farmers were lucky men. Their lives were clocked and calendered by the sun and the seasons rather than by bells and machines.

"Is that what they call a curdly sky?" Binnie asked, looking up.

"I don't know," said Packy.

"They do say that a curdly sky is the sign of rain to come in three days' time," she announced and sighed again.

Three days seemed unbearably long to wait for relief from the heat. But, in fact, Binnie had to drag herself through six more long days and nights of unrelieved heat. Her famous appetite suffered badly.

"Eat, Binnie, eat," Mrs. Howe scolded. "I'm sorry now that I ever let you go to work. Every store, every business in Lowell, everything has closed because of this awful heat. Everything except those dreadful mills. Eat, Binnie. You're falling away every day."

Binnie could not bring herself to eat no matter how many pounds she lost. Meat, milk, butter spoiled and soured almost in minutes, almost in the time between being placed on the table and picked up on the fork. And if something wasn't actually spoiled, it smelled on the edge of turning.

Because of sick stomachs, a number of women kept racing to the necessary in the mill. The time they lost from their looms and spindles was too much for Quimby. With the solemn, pompous air of a judge passing sentence, he announced: "If you are not able to work, you had better stay out all the time." He dismissed three women at once with a note in the account books that they had "worthless characters."

The others muttered with resentment. Some talked about presenting a petition of grievance to the corporation treasurer. But the heat drained too much of their energy and they did nothing.

"Cooler days are coming," the Irish sweeper said with a tired smile as she passed Binnie.

"So is Christmas," Binnie called after her. It was a feeble joke and she knew it. At least it broke the tedium of the day for a moment.

Another break in the day's work occurred in the first weaving room. One of the giant leather straps that sent power to the line shafts snapped. The looms were forced to stop. Then in the other weaving room friction heat fired two of the small belts and left charred end-pieces. Since the weaving rooms could not take any more thread, the spinning stopped. With the spinning stopped, the carding came to a halt. Room by room, floor by floor, the work backed up and the machines were closed down.

Outside, black storm clouds had at last begun collecting in a huge heavy mass. Inside the spinning room, the light turned gray and gloomy. The queer, half-drowned light, the shadow-filled room, the quieting factory scraped on some people's nerves, but Binnie rather enjoyed the strangeness. When she saw Susan's eyes rolling nervously, she offered to tell her a story. Susan and the other doffers huddled with Binnie on the floor by the window.

Binnie licked salty sweat droplets from the corner of her mouth and began. She told the story, a made-up one of her own, with great relish and many gestures. Not since Aleck left had she had such admiring attention. The first raindrops came splashing against the windowpane as she swept to a close. Then heavy rain hit the side of the building like a flapping curtain of smoke blown sideways.

In their unexpected freedom from work, the women were behaving like children let out early from school. They called out to one another across the aisles, joked and chattered in high joyous voices. One snatched at another's apron strings, pulling them untied. Her victim, laughing, chased her down the alleys, threatening to get even. Some women—those who preferred not to look out at the thundering storm—had collected at the far end. They were singing a rousing chorus of an old hymn.

A few began cleaning their stopped machines as they did at night. They had already decided there would be no more work today. It was too dark. Even if the belts were repaired instantly, nobody could see to retie the broken thread ends or work out the tangles and snarls that happened so often. Most of the petticoat lamps that hooked onto the looms and frames in the gloomy winter months had been removed by the end of March; they would not be filled with whale oil and brought back until lighting-up time in October. When the overseers came through to say everyone could go home, loud huzzahing cheers went up.

But the treat cost them. Only the dressers and weavers, who got paid by the piece, had expected their pay to run a little short. The paid-by-the-day workers were caught by surprise. After the paymaster went through on August 13, the first woman to count her money shook her fist angrily at his back.

"A day's wages held back! Blast them! We never asked to be dismissed. That was their decision, not ours. And they know full well that we worked almost the whole day. It lacked but a couple of hours to the dismissal bell. May the Devil take them all."

At home, Mrs. Howe counted Binnie's pay with a faintly unbelieving air. She stacked the coins repeatedly, changing the amount in each pile. But no amount of counting or changing of stacks could increase the total.

"Binnie, I thought your money, what you earned, would be our extra. Leeway in case of storms as your gran'pa, the captain, would have said. I planned to give you a tenth at least for yourself to do with as you pleased . . . but . . . ." She shook her head. Mama was clearly distressed. "Adam's bill of tuition comes due soon and everything has gone so dear in price. Why, a barrel of flour went up still again just last week. I shall be using every penny of this."

Mrs. Howe had not been in the habit of explaining her actions or decisions to Binnie and the long speech, which was an apology of sorts, made Binnie uncomfortable.

"I shan't miss it. Next month should bring a full pay." Binnie tried to say it casually, as if she were used to talking about such matters with her mother, but as she spoke, her heart sank.

"Thirty days hath September . . . ." had flashed into her head and the prospect of each of those days spent doing the same thing—carrying bobbin boxes back and forth, hour after hour—was a dismal one. When she thought about that endless round stretching further into October and November, her mind balked. Maybe if she counted what she had already saved, it would cheer her up.

Binnie went into the front room and reached behind the clock for her hoard. With a start she realized that the clock was stopped. Nobody in the house had noticed or complained to her about the stopped clock. Still, that was not surprising. The only time that mattered was marked off by the bells that sent her and the women in and out of the factory.

It seemed to Binnie that her life was like the clock. Stopped dead. Unmoving. Small difference how many pennies she scraped out of earnings. Like milk soured by the summer heat, the innocent dream of work and earning money had curdled for Binnie.

Small difference whether the clock started again, she decided. In a spasm of disgust, she drew back her hand, leaving the hoard untouched and the clock unwound.

12

"Don't go so fast. Besides, your end is too high up for good balance, Packy," Binnie called out to his back. She refused to say out loud that he was much taller than she or that she could not match his effort. They were carrying Florilla's domed trunk to the stagecoach depot.

This late in September, the evening light showed objects clearly but without color. Summer had drawn to a close before Florilla wrote asking for her things to be sent on. She and Frenchy had stopped finally in Niagara. Oddly enough, the place also had a grand waterfall nearby. Only the falls there were twice and twice again the size of the Pawtucket

Falls in Lowell, she wrote. (It was hard for Binnie to believe or picture the sight.) And would Mrs. Howe send along with the trunk some teas and herbs from Granny Anna, please? It was rough country out there. Doctors and good home remedies were in short supply.

Mrs. Howe had made a generous selection and stitched it all into a sailcloth bundle. Even the trunk alone was too much for Binnie to carry, so she had pressed Packy into helping. He had slung the bundle by its stout cord over one shoulder and walked in the lead carrying the front end of the trunk. Since they could not see each other's faces, conversation was awkward.

"I'm still surprised about the letter," Packy said.

"Why? Didn't you think she could write? You know the alphabet was meant for woman's use as well as man's."

"Don't be so quick to jump. You're worse than a tiger with a burning tongue who's spied a juicy calf. All I meant was so many times people go out West and nobody ever hears from them again."

"Well, she had a lot to say besides remembering herself to us all. They both got revived by some preacher out there and joined the Freedom Baptist Church. The preacher baptized them in the morning and married them in the afternoon." Binnie giggled, remembering how the women in the house had buzzed over this part of the letter. "They are cleaving together just like the Bible says. What d'you think about that Frenchy's coming out a Baptist?"

"Not much." Packy's shrug said Frenchy's abandoning the Catholics had nothing to do with him.

They reached the depot minutes after the stagecoach had

pulled in. The horses' flanks were still heaving and sweating. The baggageman hoisted the trunk onto the roof and they were free at last to walk and talk comfortably together.

Packy had so much to tell Binnie that the return trip to her house was scarcely long enough to tell it all. He looked different, older somehow, with his close-cropped hair. "Burrhead" was what the apprentices were called, he explained. They had to shave their heads or cut the hair short for safety's sake. Binnie nodded her understanding.

"That man who heads up our Works, he's so smart, Binnie," Packy declared in admiration. "Before he put together the locomotive parts last year, he had our shop copy every one. Now we got patterns to make our own instead of bringing engines from England. Major Whistler, he . . . ."

Binnie interrupted Packy. "I know that family. They have a little boy, James Abbott McNeill Whistler. He was baptized in my church. They live on Worthen Street."

Packy galloped right over the tail end of her sentence. He was too set on telling her his experiences to notice anything she had to say. All of his work in the Machine Shop excited him. Daily, they trusted him with more and more tasks; daily, he mastered some new trick or skill.

"Everybody is always trying something new in our place. Everybody pushes hard to take on more jobs. That's how you get experience." He said the last solemnly, as if offering her a new truth.

He showed her the healing scabs, the fresh raw burns, the black grease lying permanently in the creases of his knuckles. They were marks of honor to him, proof positive of his progress and learning.

152

"To watch them making a new tool out of nothing . . . out of a puddle of melted ore . . . it's magical," said Packy. "To measure, cut and shape something yourself . . . . Ah-h, I can't tell you how I feel when I see a part fits perfectly because I made it just so. . . ."

"You are a talky boy and the only one I know who can make machine work sound more beautiful than a sunset or a poem," Binnie teased him.

Packy peered at her through the deepening dusk. "But don't you think so, too?"

"Yes, if you mean it's exciting to be a maker of something new, I agree." Then she shook her head. "But if you mean that working with machines is beautiful or some marvelous privilege, uh-uh. *No.*"

"Do you dislike the machines so much then?"

"No-o-o, the machines don't bother me." Binnie spoke slowly as she tried to clear in her own mind how she felt. "I don't mind the racket so much. I dislike having to do the same mindless task over and over all day long. I just can't bring myself to get down on my knees in thanks for that kind of work."

"Well, nobody's asked you to do that," Packy said.

"Oh, yes, they practically do. Those overseers act like they're God's agents bestowing a blessing on you."

"Stuff it!" said Packy. "The mill owners and those men who run the mills worship the interest in their bank accounts more than anything else. They wouldn't hire you or anybody else if it didn't mean bigger and more profit for themselves."

"Maybe if the bosses didn't act like we're a part of the machinery, it wouldn't be so bad," Binnie continued. "The secret to being happy in the mills, I guess, is to keep your expectations low. I'm sorry. I didn't mean to sound like such a croaker."

But Packy had been caught by her problem and was not yet finished with the discussion.

"Wait, Binnie. Listen. You do your share of work for the wages, don't you? Don't ever be grateful. It's a fair exchange. Listen: My uncle has something you should read. *Address to the Workingmen* by a Seth Luther. You should read it because that author talks about these same things. If I can get my uncle to lend it, I'll bring it by your house this week. This week, I'll come by."

Binnie shifted her weight from one foot to the other. She felt nervous but determined. Good manners as well as friendship required her to say it.

"Why don't you come in the house for a minute right now? I know my mama wants to thank you."

When he had come for the trunk, he had picked up his end from the doorstep. Now Binnie saw a lively curiosity flare up in his eyes and she knew he would accept her invitation. It was a good chance to see inside a boarding house, a place he'd never been before.

Aloud, he said only, "That was a thirst-making job for sure." He paused and added with a casual air, "If I could step in for some water, I'd appreciate it."

Binnie brought him into the house warily. The only other Irish person who had crossed their threshold was Mary Kate. If Mama judged Packy by Mary Kate, Heaven knew what she might say to him. And Packy McCabe certainly would not take kindly to being treated like a backward child.

Mrs. Howe greeted them with a nod and continued toward the bedroom. A new spasm of anxiety went through Binnie. Was her mother looking for her purse? She should not, she must not. Binnie crossed her fingers tightly and made a quick silent wish. Mama was not to offer Packy any money. Friends did favors; they were not for hire to their other friends. Her mother came out of the bedroom empty-handed and Binnie gave a sigh of relief.

Mrs. Howe did not simply thank Packy for his help. She invited him to take some refreshments as well, and he accepted with a pleased smile.

"Get some mugs of that fresh fall cider, Binnie," her mother directed as she herself prepared a plate of sweets. Once Binnie saw the plate filled with rich, sweet shortbread biscuits, the kind that were reserved for company, she relaxed completely. She did not have to be ashamed of either her mother or her friend in this, their first meeting.

When Maria came into the kitchen, Binnie introduced her with a flourish, enjoying the way Packy's eyes widened in appreciation. Dorcas came right behind Maria and examined Packy with interest until she realized he wasn't full grown.

"Still, he's a good-looker," she said loudly to Maria. Then, addressing Packy himself, she asked, "You must have lots of family, an Irisher like you? Any big brothers like yourself at home?"

When he answered politely that he was an only child, Binnie winced at Dorcas's visible surprise. Packy, who had quickly covered his mouth with one hand, rolled laughing eyes at Binnie. Dorcas had wound her hair tightly in paper curlers, so tightly that her sandy eyebrows were pulled up more than an inch. She looked like a Medusa with the many curlers snaking all over her head.

155

Binnie avoided Packy's eyes as she tried to answer Dorcas's next question with a straight face. "News at the Post Office? Well, everybody was heated up, talking about the premium system. Some say that the Hamilton Company will be putting it in by October."

"The premium system? Why, what d'they mean? No matter if we do want to earn more, those old looms can't be speeded up to get any more yardage out of them. They'd break down completely. Not to mention us operators. We'd be frazzled."

"You've got it all mixed up, Dorcas. The premium is *not to us*. And it's not the machinery that gets speeded up. It's the operators," Phoebe Little corrected.

Her sister Grace added helpfully, "The *overseer* gets the premium. The one who gets his girls to produce the most work each week is rewarded. He is given a cash bonus. I believe some use that system down Waltham way."

Mrs. Howe who had been reading a letter from Cousin Cornelia, looked up with a frown. "With the result that every overseer is encouraged to work all the girls much harder yet?"

"I hope that what you have heard is not so, Binnie." Maria spoke slowly. She had a look of distaste on her face. "The whole smacks too much of the cotton fields. We're not ignorant field slaves to be whipped to greater efforts."

"I should say not!" Maria's comment had moved Phoebe out of her usual ladylike calm. She actually sputtered as she talked. "We come from . . . from as good . . . and the same stock as any free man in America."

"That would not and does not change the fact that the

156

premium system is already in effect in some other factories," Maria pointed out to Phoebe with flat logic.

Phoebe sniffed delicately, like someone who has caught a whiff of garbage. She shook her head.

"But no. Not Lowell," she said. "Lowell is the model for the whole world. Everyone looks to us for the latest in progress and technology. Besides, you know how they designed the whole with the houses and rules, all of it for the workers' sakes. Never! They'll never put in a system that does not have a care for the workers first and for their health. The owners cannot afford such a system here, for they cannot afford to lose the world's good opinion of them."

By the end of this speech, Phoebe had regained her calm. She had at least convinced herself. Binnie was not so sure that Phoebe was right, and the look in Packy's eyes suggested he wasn't, either.

Her doubts came flooding back when she saw the visitors who came to the mills the following week. Quimby led two from the group into Spinning Room Number 2. At the sight of them, a woman who had been swiping at her dirt-stained face with her arm ducked around and hid behind the end of her spinning frame. Her quick movement reminded Binnie of the mouse, Harriet Stanton-Smith.

But these two men were not husbands hunting for runaway wives. They were prosperous businessmen dressed so alike as to be almost in a uniform. Both wore long-tailed mulberry-colored coats with narrow notched lapels. Both had starched white snowfalls of cravat tied around the neck. They took off their high, shiny beaver hats and made courteous half-bows to the room at large. Thereafter, they ignored the women completely. They talked to one another, asked questions of Quimby, listened intently and began arguing between themselves. One of them raised his arm as if he were counting the number of spindles on a frame. That was when the first faint alarm went through Binnie. They passed by her on the way out. The snatches of conversation that she heard sounded strangely like echoes.

". . . we cannot afford to replace . . . but the heavier machines would speed up the . . . . We cannot afford new costs. . . . If the work assignments are enlarged. . . . We cannot afford to overlook . . . ."

Cannot afford.

Her own mother lying in bed that night used the same phrase.

"Honest people cannot afford to buy anything today. Prices are wicked and getting worse. Binnie, I'm ashamed to say it but I'm almost glad that Cornelia is keeping Aleck until Christmas. That's one less mouth for me to worry about and it means you can keep on working, though I still think you belong in school. Every little bit helps at a time like this."

Mama gave the pillow a hard jab and turned over, putting her head in the new hollow. Suddenly her voice came again out of the darkness.

"But I will not feed those girls milk toast. They cannot live on sops. We must get an increase in our board money somehow. We must. Go to sleep quickly, Binnie," she commanded, just as if she had not been the one whose talk was keeping Binnie awake.

Binnie imagined that boarding women all over town had been talking to themselves in the night. Certainly they had all stiffened their resolution. By the end of the week, they presented their remonstrances in writing to the corporations. The corporations all agreed: Food costs had clearly risen; board payments had not. The directors took steps speedily to remedy the situation. The notice was posted on the following Monday.

～13

Binnie didn't stop to read the notice. She pulled ahead of the mob clattering down the stairs. Then she broke into a sprint and shot first through the gates. On these September days of fast-fading twilight, she liked to take a roundabout way home. The solitary walk through the little woods gave her a chance to hunt for some late aster blooms and to sniff at a lucky find of witch hazel with yellow flowers and brown nuts on the same twig. It gave her a chance to feel as if she belonged to herself.

Coming up to the house, she could hear through the open windows the women buzzing loudly. She wondered what it would be like to come into a totally empty house. In the kitchen Mama was slicing cold corned beef, bringing the knife down with loud angry whacks. Binnie stood still for a moment, confused. She wasn't so late, was she? Why were the corners of her mother's mouth pulled down and tucked in tightly?

Binnie cleared her throat. She cautiously offered a remark.

"I hear the corporation put out a new notice about the board monies," she said.

"Yes, they certainly did." Mrs. Howe shoved away a platter full of meat and new sour pickles. It skidded dangerously close to the edge of the table.

"They did increase the money, didn't they?" Binnie asked anxiously. She searched her memory for scraps of remarks heard on the way out of the mill. She thought that she'd even heard a figure. "Won't you be getting twenty-five cents a week more for each boarder? Isn't that what you wanted?"

"Don't you talk so foolishly about what you don't know, you silly girl. They've robbed Peter to pay Paul and you want me to be happy about it? Just take the meat in there and don't talk to me again, d'you hear?"

Mama's face was as flushed as when she had been sick. Binnie clamped her lips together with a silent vow. She would not say a single word. Not to Mama, not to anybody. Or at least not until she had heard or figured out what was wrong.

The conversation when she sat down gave her no clues. The women were talking about a story from the newspapers. Someone had died. An Aaron Burr who had once been vice-president of the United States. From the way they spoke, the man had done some less respectable things as well. Binnie's head shot up when she heard the words "treason" and "murder." She was even more surprised to hear her mother defending him.

"There's only so much a soul can take, you know," said Mrs. Howe. "If you had endured that poor man's history...."

Binnie was surprised by Mama's defense and wondered what the true history of his life was. She guessed that Mama might have some clippings about him and resolved to look in the scrapbook after supper.

"He was provoked unbearably by Alexander Hamilton. It was a fair duel, and he himself might have been killed. I do think that Burr paid dearly for his sins thereafter."

"And his lechery? You forgive him those sins as well? For he was a womanizer. There's no denying that." Phoebe spoke with a haughty lift to her eyebrows.

"I won't deny that. But he's not the first and won't be the last man who likes women too much," Mrs. Howe answered.

"Not like our dear employers. Nobody will ever accuse *them* of liking women too much." The words came from a source that surprised Binnie. Porky-Dorky had spoken them with an angry toss of her head.

Mama, who had been on her way out, stopped short at the doorway. She put her hands up and then dropped them in a helpless what-can-I-do gesture. "When we asked for relief on account of the inflation of our costs, nobody ever dreamed they would take the road they have. It's unfair. Unjust. Why, I'd rather be purse-pinched all the days of my life than have them extract the increase from your wages."

Mrs. Howe's dismay had the effect of a thunderclap on the women. Like overfilled clouds, they burst all in one instant.

"Why should they abuse us so? . . . They cannot do this to us. . . . Well, they are . . . hardly enough to live on now . . . ."

"Why didn't they take more out of the men's wages?

They make more money than we do, they eat more than we and their boarding women must need a greater relief still . . . ."

"Twelve and a half cents less every week. Gone. It's unconscionable of them to take that money from us." Even the gentle Grace had been moved to complain.

The one dollar and twenty-five cents that each woman owed for a week's board was taken out in the countinghouse. The operatives never even saw that money, though it counted as part of their wages. Now to reduce further the sum that had been going directly into their pockets would cause hardship.

"Now . . . now when times are hard, we must expect . . . ." The widow Penfield, who did not read the newspapers or think too deeply about any subject, struggled to find an acceptable end to her sentence.

"That's a lie." To Binnie's amazement, she heard herself cutting into the widow's statement. "Sales are booming. Times are not hard . . . for them! I heard Quimby say they have more markets for goods at better prices than ever before."

"But, my dear, you can't expect them to take away from the profits of the shareholders."

"Why not?" Binnie asked. She felt perverse and contrary enough at this point to challenge Kirk Boott himself.

"Binnie's right," Maria said. "Shareholders are expected to bear the burden of the costs in a manufactory. That's what entitles them to a share of the profits. They're quick enough to put out their hands and collect their returns. Let them be just as quick to cover the increased expenses and cost of the management from their own pockets. They should not be putting that burden on those who can least afford to carry it." Maria's words were typical of her cool and reasonable self, but the last sentence came out louder than usual.

"We have been walking all around the truth and at quite a distance, too. No amount of talking can disguise what this means. It means, plainly and simply, a wage cut for us all." Dorcas's gravelly voice had deepened to a growl.

"You could take on an extra loom," Grace offered hesitantly. "You're the ablest weaver on the floor."

There was silence for a moment as the whole table considered this.

"Work twice as hard in order to make the same as I used to?" Dorcas snorted in contempt. "Thanks for nothing."

In a loud voice that commanded their attention, Binnie said, "In the Greek myths, King Tantalus stands in water up to his chin. But he is constantly thirsty because whenever he bends to drink, the waters recede. And fruits hang ripe on the trees, but he's always hungry because they hang just out of reach."

She paused, a little astonished at herself. For someone who had vowed not to say a word, she seemed to be doing more than a share of the talking this night. Yet no one had interrupted her; no one had called her a saucy child or told her to be quiet. They listened so intently that she boldly finished the comparison which had sprung into her mind. "Doesn't that story sound like an echo of our problem?"

"The girl has pointed out the truth of the matter. For all the talk about the fruits of technology, we don't get to taste any of them. Only work and still more work," Maria observed wryly.

"That's right. For another thing, there's all that talk about those grand new labor-saving machines. Whose labor is saved? Not mine. Not when they keep hounding me to speed up." A fat, freckle-faced newcomer who shared the widow's room had found the courage to contribute to the conversation.

"If we permit this, Heaven knows what they'll foist on us next time," said Maria.

"We have little choice. It behooves us to remember that we are ladies and to act accordingly. With dignity," Phoebe Little said.

The widow Penfield nodded in agreement. She tugged her ever-sliding shawl back up on her shoulders and tried to look wise. "You don't bite the hand that feeds you."

"No, but when that hand doesn't feed you very well, you better do something. Or resign yourself to starve, and I for one don't intend to do that," Dorcas snapped back.

Mrs. Howe brought up the point that had bothered her from the start. "I don't understand the corporation. It's not as if they don't already make sizeable profits from the sale of their goods. They can well afford to shoulder the rising costs. There should be no need to take another twelve and a half cents from you girls. If they really cared as they claim, that would be the right and proper thing to do."

"We can't know the reasons for their decisions. We are out of our sphere when we attempt to speak against them. These are men's matters to be decided by men," said Phoebe. For her, that closed the subject completely.

Binnie was disgusted. That Phoebe would help to cut off her own nose and then argue that her face looked better that way. Binnie spoke up again, deliberately raising her voice to make it childish and questioning.

"Out of our sphere? But who ordains our sphere? Does Kirk Boott do that? I thought God was supposed to do it."

Her mother shot her a sharp look. She had not missed the sting to Binnie's supposedly innocent question. Nor had some of the others, judging from the snickers.

Phoebe retreated to her original statement. "We must never lose our dignity. We must act with dignity. That is the most precious part of our character as ladies."

"Well, I can't eat my dignity," said Dorcas. She was almost choked with anger. "We must do something."

"What can we do?" The freckle-faced girl sounded as young and lost as Aleck when he cried in the dark, Binnie thought.

"Ask around. Ask the girls over to the other corporations what's doing there. Think on it. Sleep on it," Mrs. Howe advised.

The murmur of agreement fell quickly away as the women left the supper table. Binnie watched them scattering, each to her own affairs. She could not recall ever seeing them so silent. Mrs. Howe's advice had been good and practical. It was not her fault that Binnie's dreams took the direction that they did that night.

Except for finding Quimby at her side, the beginning of the dream was pleasurable enough. They sat at a table with countless platters of smoked oysters, a delicacy that Binnie loved. In life she never got to eat enough of them, but in the dream the platters, full to heaping, stretched all the way down the long table. Quimby had made a prompt start, popping the smoky-sweet, plump tidbits into his mouth. Binnie stretched out her hand and had almost gotten an oyster to her mouth when with a thrill of horror she saw that the brown, velvety oyster contained a woman's face. More, the face was alive and twisted with weeping. She turned over oyster after oyster, first from one platter and then from another. Oyster after oyster, they all turned into women weeping. Frantically, she tugged at Quimby's arm to stop him. But he only smiled, patted her on the head and went on eating. Worst of all, she still had a passionate longing to join Quimby in eating the oysters.

When Binnie woke, she herself was weeping. She went off to work that morning with only a mug of tea for breakfast. She could not bring herself to put anything in her mouth that required chewing.

Although she was early, others had collected at the locked gates earlier still. Binnie frowned at the thick clots of waiting women. Were they so anxious to make an early start? Did they truly hope to offset the cut by speeding themselves up? More and more of them pressed closer and closer.

On all sides, Binnie heard sentences beginning with "They say . . . ." These were interrupted constantly by others saying "What we ought to do is . . . ." The women, she realized, were not simply waiting for the starting bell. Rather, they were holding a meeting of sorts, pooling their knowledge and sharing ideas.

The watchman appeared to open the gates and the women fell silent. All day long, a sense of urgent need pushed them to leave the machines for hurried moments of talk and gestures. Whenever any man came near enough to watch or hear them, the women retreated into standing alone and still, each by her frame. These sudden retreats and silences, oddly enough, carried more threat of a storm ahead than when their heads bent close together in talk.

Binnie worked in a state of prickly awareness. By afternoon, the bubbles of uneasiness surfaced into outright trouble. One overseer, made jolly by his noonday hard cider, clapped a spinner on the back saying; "That's a good girl. Start 'er right up. You know the old proverb, 'Get thy spindle and thy distaff ready and God will send you the flax.'"

She jerked her shoulder away from him and answered sharply, "But who will send the silver to pay me for my labor? You people refuse to pay an honest wage for an honest day's work. Maybe I should apply to Satan?"

First he sputtered and then he roared. All joviality gone, he dismissed her on the spot for "disorderly conduct and mutiny."

Behind him, a woman said loudly, "Satan might be a better boss indeed than some we could name."

He whirled around and dismissed that one for "levity and impudence." All around him the women hissed. Their shocked, angry whispers sounded like rain approaching over the top of a hill. He stared around with a surprised look. He could not dismiss the whole room of women. Angry and defeated, he stalked out to tell Quimby in the counting room.

Supper that night was the noisiest that Binnie ever remembered. The women were talking over the events in Spinning Room Number 2 and sharing what knowledge and rumors they had picked up from girls in the other mills.

Dorcas's gravelly voice, louder than any, captured their attention. "The weavers over to the Hamilton Corporation are thinking and talking about forming a combination."

"You mean a combination like a trade union? Like the kind of association that men form? I never heard of such a thing," said Grace.

"I should think such a thing is improper, if not immoral, for women to engage in," said Phoebe. "Besides, it will be a cold day in Hell before so many hundreds of women can come to agreement."

"I don't see why you say that. If we can feel the bonds of sisterhood enough to help one another at work as we do, it seems to me that we can unite for some future benefit," said Maria.

"But what exactly can a combination do for us now?" said Binnie, feeling very practical. "We need to make plain to the directors and the superintendents of the companies that we disapprove of what they're doing to us."

Maria answered, "For one thing, those in it might agree to ring each mill. If no other woman entered to work for shame of breaking the bonds of sisterhood, that would plainly say we all think this cut a disgrace."

"Maybe so," said Mrs. Howe. "Of course, first you have to persuade everybody to turn out of the mills. They tried that a couple of years ago in the winter of '34 and it gained them nothing then."

"They did? A real turn-out? I don't remember it," said Binnie.

"No surprise that you don't," said Mrs. Penfield. The widow was one of the few women present who had been in Lowell back then. "It didn't last but a day or two and not many joined it. Seems to me there were not above five or six hundred girls taking part in it."

"Which tells us that everybody, absolutely everybody, has to go out in the same instant from every mill building. To have an effect, the turn-out must stop the work of the mills," Dorcas concluded. Her voice had a bitter edge as she added, "Then the owners would take us seriously."

Later, as Binnie and Mrs. Howe washed dishes, Binnie asked her mother what she thought about the day's happening.

"Bad conscience," said her mother. "Bad conscience made that man jump too fast." Mama looked at Binnie with frowning concentration and a measuring eye. "That skirt is way too short. And that waist looks skimpy. Too skimpy. You have grown both up and out this summer. More than I expected. I think we had better plan on two new dresses this fall besides letting down your Sunday dress for everyday wear."

The Binnie of last spring would have whooped with joy at what had been said. The words would have supplied her with enough pleasure to last a week or more. Now the important moment slid by, flattened out by her pressing need to settle some disturbing questions.

She had felt the tug of sisterhood that Maria talked about and she agreed completely with Dorcas's conclusion. On the other hand, she wasn't so sure about a union that required acts of disobedience like walking out of work. She had read the book from Packy's uncle. It had told her that many—especially businessmen and the authorities—considered combinations or union of workers illegal and dangerous conspiracies.

"Mama, if there is a turn-out, what ought I to do?"

"To do?" Her mother stopped abruptly in her tracks.

"Yes, what ought I to do? They say that anyone who turns out will be blacklisted for all their lives all over the country. They will be tagged as troublemakers, not to be hired by anyone. And, of course, you know . . . no work means no money."

There was a long silence while her mother looked at her. She seemed confused by the question and Binnie's heart sank. She had hoped for a quick, decisive answer from her mother. Mrs. Howe sat down with shoulders hunched. She chewed on her lower lip and still did not answer Binnie.

Finally, she muttered aloud, "It means more than . . . . They could . . . they could go so far as to cancel . . . out of the house. Where would we go? You know"—here she looked directly at Binnie—"we'll have to be here facing up to what's been done long after it's over."

Mrs. Howe nodded to herself. She had reached a conclusion but for once she did not move briskly. She stood up slowly as if her bones ached.

"Binnie, there comes a time when you have to decide things for yourself. I just don't know. I'm not there in the mills. If you're old enough to do the work and hold down the job, you're old enough to work out the right and wrong of this for yourself. In the end, you have to be accountable to yourself. Not to me, not to your friends, but accountable to yourself and to what you understand is the right. You decide. I can't tell you what to do in this, Binnie."

Binnie, who had chafed at being a child, who had fretted over having to obey her mother's commands, discovered now that there was something worse—being given the right to take charge of your own life.

She found herself shivering. Not with cold, for the room was too warm for that. It was a shiver of fright that started with a shake of the head, trembled down through her body and contracted her very toes. How could she, Binnie, make a decision that might turn them out of this house?

Just as suddenly, rage flooded through her and Binnie found herself hotter than she could bear. It was her mother's business to make decisions for the family. How dare she quit at this crucial moment? How dare she thrust upon Binnie such an impossible task?

In a mix of equal parts of fear and rage, Arabinia J. Howe flung herself out of the kitchen to find refuge in the little woods. She had never been so lonely in all her twelve years.

14

October 1, 1836.

Four abreast, the front line held firm. Marchers from Merrimack Mill Number 1 moved steadily though unevenly across the mill yard. Women darted in almost every direction like minnows in a cool stream. Behind the front line, the rows shifted. The lines swelled out into bowed curves, broke and re-formed. The marchers fluttered bright-colored scarves and waved calashes high over their heads, beckoning others to join them.

High above them, the evenly spaced windows were crowded with watchers. They peered through and over the tops of the plants that jammed every window sill. The gauzy green curtains of leaves and the sunlight winking against the windows made it difficult to see.

Neither group could pick out the separate faces of friends, but the watchers could hear plainly the ragged chorus of the marchers' song. It was a parody, a play on the words of a well-known song about a nun.

Oh, isn't it a pity such a pretty girl as I
Should be sent to the factory to pine away and die?
Oh! I will not be a slave
For I'm so fond of liberty
That I cannot be a slave.

"Slaves, that's right! That's all we are. White slaves."

"That abolitionist who came here . . . remember him? The one who got pelted with stones by the Town Hall? He was right when he called this town 'Low-Hell'!"

The bitter remarks popped with explosive force from somewhere within the core of the watchers.

"Ladies, ladies. What kind of behavior is this?" From the far end of the room came Franklin Quimby's voice. He had entered the room unnoticed and was shouting at them. "Ladies, where is your moral sense? To abandon your work in this shameless way? You should not dignify that rabble below with a second glance."

"Mister Quimby, that rabble, as you call it, has my sister in it. If they *look* like rabble, the fault lies with your wages, not with them." A woman with the bold dark looks of a gypsy challenged him.

"What more do you women want? You know full well that even as the cloth is being made, so too your whole characters are elevated and improved by the privileges and discipline of the factory life. Doesn't that count for aught with you?" Quimby looked more than ever like a disagreeable Roman emperor, the tip of his long nose quivering in anger.

"Ha! Next you'll be wanting us *to pay* for the privilege of working in these smelly, filthy-dirty, ill-making places," one of the women shouted back at him.

"Any right-thinking woman who values her character should be happy to do so if asked," Quimby shot back.

This pompous foolishness was too much for the women. Half a dozen or more booed and hissed.

The handsome dark woman shouted, "Save your nonsense for those who like to eat pompous pie." She stepped forward and turned to address the others. "Isn't it enough that the corporation dictates to us where we are to eat, sleep and pray? Must we listen now to lectures on how to think, too? I won't grovel to this worm for my dollars. Let's go. Our sisters are waiting." With an angry wave, she headed for the door.

Binnie Howe knew that willy-nilly she had to make a choice: to go or to stay. The need to decide was so strong that she could feel it between her shoulder blades like a giant's hand pushing. Her stomach gave one sharp, threatening lurch and then settled itself. There was a finality to this moment like nothing she had ever experienced before. Binnie took a single step forward and then another. She stopped. She held out her hands.

"Will you row in the same boat with us?" she asked the doffer who stood on one side of her. Her voice was deep but sounded hollow to her own ears. Without looking to see who or how many joined her, she moved briskly to the doorway.

Floor by floor, the mill was emptying out. The trickle of

women became a flood so great that it clogged up the stairs. Binnie, who had made it to the bottom, was wiggling her way out to the lines of women. Her eyes searched to see if anyone from her house had joined the marchers.

One row short of the front line, she found Dorcas Boomer and Maria Teasdale. They pulled her between them and linked arms with her. Binnie was almost lifted off her feet and carried along. If it seemed strange to find herself lined up and linked with Dorcas Boomer, the feeling of being in the right place was even stronger. Binnie raised her voice to sing: "Oh, I will not be a slave . . . ."

Over and over the verses were repeated. Appleton, Hamilton . . . every corporation was visited, and in mill after mill women walked out. The winding procession grew longer and fatter. Five hundred, six hundred, nine hundred.

Binnie looked over her shoulder in awe. The end was nowhere in sight. There must be a thousand women in this together, she thought. No, more than a thousand. She corrected herself as she caught sight of another bulge coming around the corner. Through the din of singing and shuffling, stomping feet, she heard dogs barking and children cheering. She heard, too, her own name being called. Even before she saw the caller, she knew it would be Packy McCabe. He had been running alongside and finally found her.

"You! Hey, Skinny Binnie. Good spunk, girl! I knew you were a front runner," he shouted at her and laughed.

Somewhere he had picked up a battered kettle. With a big stick, he banged on the kettle in a steady beat that helped the marchers to keep step. He was not the only one. Others were clanging pots and lids together like cymbals. A marching band could not have made a braver noise. On both sides of the march, townspeople had lined up: some to cheer, some to tut-tut. Since she didn't have a hand free to wave, Binnie waggled her chin and bobbed her head up and down to show him she had heard. The joy inside her was a waterfall spilling over in a grand splashing shower of goodwill toward everyone. She smiled at the disapproving faces of the Seavy twins who watched from the sidelines. Binnie felt that she could march forever.

The end came at Chapel Hill. The lines broke and the women milled about in some confusion. After a final clanging and banging, silence of a sort settled on the crowd. They eyed one another uncertainly. A young woman clambering up on a turned-over keg captured Binnie's attention.

In a clear soprano voice, the woman called out, "Sisters." Again and again she called until everybody had turned toward her.

"We have only just begun. Some have failed to join us. They are blind. They do not see that we have every reason to be confident of triumph. Yet we must claim our rights to the fruits of our labor, our right to justice and mercy for *all* in the band of sisterhood. Remember: In Union there is power. And we must have, we will have the power to press for and win a decent wage. If we organize ourselves to stand fast . . . if we hold out and if we stay out all together, we will prevail. To participate in public protest is not enough. We must organize."

A day ago, the sight of a woman orating about justice on Chapel Hill would have seemed a freaky oddity. On this extraordinary day, it was simply a fitting end to the events. But the meaning of her words shook Binnie, who had screwed up all her courage to meet the challenge of making a decision. It had not occurred to her that there would be something more to face. That, in fact, a successful end to the turn-out required still more steps to be taken.

"Hear! *Hear!* True, too true. . . ."

Through the huzzahs and clapping, the practical ones had already begun the planning: how to persuade the remaining operatives to join them, how to form an association, when to meet again all together. Binnie's mind had moved ahead to consider the task looming before her: to go home and face her mother. She dreaded it.

"Binnie can."

"Binnie can wh-what?" she asked in a startled squeak as the hand fell on her shoulder.

"Go from house to house to tell women of the meeting place and time that the committee fixes on," said Dorcas. "It has to be done speedily."

"Well, I can get to all the boarding houses in half an hour or less," Binnie answered. She felt proud and a little smug to be included in the planned actions.

Going home, she wondered uneasily how her mother would feel and began practicing explanations. All the carefully chosen and rehearsed words flew out of Binnie's mind when she saw her mother's face. She blurted out her defense pell-mell.

"There wasn't any way I could stay in, Mama. No way. The corporation is so unfair. It's not just the wages. It's everything. Everything. You know the hours are too long and the way they treat people like machinery. They're so unfair . . . unjust . . . ." Her voice trailed off. "Mama," she started again miserably. "Mama, I'm sorry about losing you the money of my wages. I'm sorry, but I couldn't stay in."

Her mother let out her breath in a long sigh. "I might have known."

There was a wrinkly frown between her eyes but her mouth was soft with the corners turning up. It was a half-and-half face: half-worried, half-proud.

"I told you, Binnie, to decide for yourself. I'm not going to complain now that you did. We've lived a good many years without wages from you. I suppose we can do it again somehow. You're right. If you stay in, you're telling the corporation that they have the right to treat people any way they choose for the sake of their profits. So long as what you've done don't scare or haunt you later."

"It would scare me more *not* to go out," said Binnie.

It was true. Binnie thought of all the childish fears that used to haunt her and smiled. Ghosts. Indians. The dark. None was so real or so awful as the thought of how she would feel if she had not joined the protest.

Her mother said no more about Binnie's decision, but the next morning Binnie awakened to hear Mrs. Howe bargaining hard for the farmer's culls, the same ones she had scorned earlier. She had finished pickling and preserving the winter's pantry supplies in September but now she started a new batch of preserves. And she dismissed Mary Kate for the time being.

The bells rang as usual but only three women from the house left to report for work. They went out accompanied by dark looks and mutterings from those who stayed home.

"Tonight we must persuade them to hold out with us," said Maria. "No time now for reproaches or quarrels. We have much to do."

She had received already from the committee tasks for

all. Binnie was to go from house to house informing everyone of the formation of the Factory Girls Association.

"Judging from the numbers we had with us yesterday, you should find at least one girl in every house who is already in sympathy. Bring back the names of those who volunteer to sign up members and collect dues for the Association," Maria told her.

Binnie left the house humming in a lighthearted way. She felt good. Up and down the block she went with her message, avoiding only the brick tenements where the overseers lived with their families.

At Susan's house, she saw the first wagon. The center was piled high with baggage and the side seat planks crowded with women.

Bewildered, Binnie asked, "But where is everybody going today?"

"Home, girl," one of the women called down to her.

"But why?"

"Why? Because I'm tired of being treated like dirt scraped out of the barnyard. Because I never planned to live my whole life in Lowell."

"Wait, though. There's an Association been formed to support our cause."

"If it does any good, I'll hear it soon enough back home. I may or may not come back. Depending. We'll see."

Elly Tompkins, the music-loving student of the piano, brushed past Binnie, handed a carpetbag up to a woman and climbed up herself.

"Elly, you've only just come and you said that this time you were staying," said Binnie, tugging at Elly's hem.

Elly, recognizing Binnie, answered apologetically, "I

178

meant to. But since all my friends have turned out, I can't go in to work and I don't have enough savings laid up to live idly. If I don't go home now, I won't have the money to pay my way home later."

Binnie gave a halfhearted wave as the wagon pulled away. When she returned home, she was not surprised to find a pile of baggage in the front entry. She wondered only whose it was and how many were leaving. In the front room, Grace was finishing a speech about taking advantage of the time out to visit their nephew in Springfield, while Phoebe was assuring everyone that the Littles would be back among their good friends before long.

"How do you expect to get on? Assuming the mills open fully, do you think the Merrimack will take you in again?" asked Mrs. Howe.

"But, my dear, we had to safeguard our good name and protect our characters. We gave the required two weeks' notice, of course," said Phoebe. Realizing suddenly what she had said, she reddened and went out the door abruptly.

"Why, that means she gave notice the day they first posted the news about the new board rate," said Binnie indignantly. "She's never risked a thing. All the while since we turned out, she's known she could come back any time. What a sneak! And she's always so righteous."

"Just because she's righteous doesn't mean she cares about the right of a cause or the rights of others. There is a difference," said Maria.

Although it made no sense, Binnie felt a personal guilt over every wagon that she saw leaving. Each time, she felt that it was her fault somehow that those women had not been convinced to stay. As the week drew to a close, she realized with alarm that the trickle of operatives leaving Lowell was daily growing larger.

Those women who stayed recognized that they had to keep their solidarity or the corporations would ignore them. They agreed that the officers of the Factory Girls Association should speak for all of them and pledged money from the dues to support those sisters who had no savings put by.

Binnie carried the news of the pledge around town with great relief. She expected that it would stem the tide of outgoing women. Packy caught up with her as she came out of the last house on the Hamilton Corporation. He was grinning and waving a newspaper clipping.

"Something to make you feel good," he said, handing her the clipping. "The Lynn *Record* sure agrees with you all. They call the bosses 'aristocratic and offensive employers.' How d'ya like that?"

"Well, whoopee pickle! Just fine," Binnie said with satisfaction. Quickly, before he left, she asked, "You got any other news?"

"The men have been saying it's your fight mostly, but that we all want and need reasonable hours and a decent wage. Anyway, I think they're taking a resolution of support to the National Trades' Union convention. Maybe the delegates will pass it, maybe even vote some money to help. They figure that will give you a good account in the press. A good press is important, you know, to gain the sympathy of outsiders."

"But a lot of the newspapers just don't like unions," said Binnie. "They're dishonest, too. The papers never quarrel about all the other combinations. Only the workingmen's."

"What other kind is there, for Heaven's sake?"

Binnie had been brooding about this for some time. "You don't think the companies are in a combination, a union of their own? Didn't you know that Henry Hall, who's treasurer for the Tremont, is also the same for the Suffolk and Lawrence? It's so much harder to win a change if the same people serve as owners and officers of all the different corporations. Add to that the way they all write around and agree among themselves about lowering the wages, fixing the house rules and circulating that wormy blacklist, and I say that's a conspiracy and combination just as much as any other. Worse! It's an abomination of a combination."

Packy laughed at her last sentence and her furiously waving arms. "You look like a windmill," he told her. "I see what you mean, though. That's a good point you made. Maybe they'll talk about that, too, at the convention. It's coming at the end of this month, or early on next."

"November is a long time to wait," said Binnie. "Especially for a maybe-benefit."

Because she had carried the figures from the women back to the committee, Binnie knew how much had been accomplished in a week. On the first day of the turn-out, 386 women and three sympathetic men had walked out of the Lawrence Corporation. The day after that, the number jumped to 450, a good third of all their workers. More than a thousand women had signed up already as members of the Association.

"Still," Packy argued, "a resolution of support is worth something. It makes you all more respectable. I have to beat it. Tomorrow is a 'specially busy work day for me," he said, turning to leave.

"No busier than mine," Binnie said with feeling. "These

last days I've been doing more running than when I carried bobbin boxes. See you tomorrow after supper."

It was true. Before, after and in between her household chores, she traveled constantly, carrying the drafts of resolutions, lists of names and messages through a network of striking operatives and their committees.

She carried home Packy's clipping and added it to her growing collection. From the day of the turn-out, she had begun collecting all the newspapers that she could find. Every night she read and reread the accounts of the strike, the state of the textile industry and even the affairs in the capital. As a messenger, she felt obliged to keep herself informed of the whole.

"Against this rise in the price of the board the female operatives are now remonstrating," said the Lowell *Courier*. "We believe there is but one opinion and this is that the turn-outs are wrong and their employers right."

"Wrong! Wrong! Wrong!" Every single "wrong" was accompanied by a loud bang. Binnie had finished pasting the cutting in Mama's scrapbook by pounding it with her fist.

"Well, the paper is certainly wrong about there being only one opinion," her mother observed with dry amusement.

"The editor who wrote that must be dead between the ears. Just because we don't have big tall smokestacks pouring out ugly black smoke on the town, just because the overseers don't beat the children, he thinks we have no claim of a just cause."

Maria and Dorcas, who were bringing dirty dishes into the kitchen, stopped. Dorcas opened her mouth to say something, but Binnie was too passionately angry now to stop and listen.

"And those visitors who come here .... They look at the nice brick buildings with the flowers out front and at our pet plants in the windows. Then they *ohh-hh* and *ahh-hh* as if we worked in some kind of pleasure palace. Everybody from outside always says our factory system is the best thing that ever happened in America. And they're always turning their noses up at the English factories because they got 'lower classes' working there. Well, did you know their 'lower classes' have got more rights than we do now? It's against the law for the factories over there to work children more than sixty-nine hours a week. Ask them, just ask them here to do the same and see what you get." Binnie's voice deepened to mimic the directors who had visited the mill. "*Garrumph.* We uh . . . can't afford to . . . . Moral poppycock and hogwash! That's what I say!"

"Bravo, Binnie Howe." Maria's applause made Binnie jump and blush. "That was grand. As good a speech as any that Daniel Webster ever delivered. You know I'm one of those delegated to go the rounds of the mill buildings? To assail and persuade those girls who are left to join us. I'll take any help or advice you can give me gladly, for you know, I'm not such a good speaker."

"Where are you aiming for? Who do you plan to address first?" Dorcas asked her.

"Why, I had no particular scheme in mind."

"You should. The warpers. There's only a handful of them in each building. We catch the warpers. If we get all of them, it's better even than getting a big quantity of women. With all of one kind of worker gone out—especially warpers —the work will be stoppered up. Blocked. The whole mill will have to close down."

Brilliant! Binnie gave Dorcas a surprised and approving look. Really, she had worked out a very sensible strategy. A few short weeks ago, Binnie would not have dreamed she could like Dorcas half so well as she did now.

The planning did have an effect. The Hamilton Corporation was so short of help by the end of the second week that it closed one mill completely. The few workers left had to be shifted to the other two mills on the corporation. Those corporations which, like the Tremont, were struggling to operate with only one-half of their hands, placed advertisements in newspapers all over New England for "better-behaved women" to replace the walkouts. That second Sunday some of the ministers preached sermons about the immorality of women who combined and conspired against the corporations.

With the end nowhere in sight, more women reluctantly decided they could not afford to use up any more of their savings. They packed their bags. More carts, wagons and carriages left Lowell, carrying these women away. To Binnie's dismay, when the carts and wagons clattered and creaked back into town, they did not return empty. They were filled with women from remote farms in the countryside, from hamlets in Vermont, from the villages and mountains of New Hampshire, all eager replacements for those who had left.

Watching the procession of wagons from her front window, Binnie scowled. "Nobsticks. Strike breakers. Traitors," she growled angrily. She knew it was childish, but it relieved her feelings to call the newcomers names.

"What can you expect? They never earned a penny where they were, so even the less amount looks good to them. They're hungry for hard cash," said Dorcas with a sour sadness.

Binnie felt a guilty shame for both the women and for herself. It was not so long ago that she had burned equally with a hunger for money. Of all things, it was the least important to her now.

"Cheer up," said Maria, who had come to the window. "It's the end that counts. If everyone listens to what we have to say, they're bound to see the issue as we do. That's why I've come looking for you, Binnie. There's a rally planned for two days hence to drum up support. No, don't go yet." Maria checked Binnie's departure with a raised hand. "I wanted to ask, too, if you'd give me a hand later with this speech that I'm to make. Since you've been studying up on this, you may have some fresher thoughts than I and you have a good, telling way of making points."

Binnie was gratified that Maria considered her help worth having and was encouraged by the proposed rally. Perhaps so many women massed together in a common cause would convince those Boston merchants to act like the Christian philanthropists they claimed to be. Perhaps. But doubt like a rat nibbling cheese sat in a corner of her mind.

 15

"... verminous ... vice-ridden ...."

The voice echoed up the stair like the hollow splash of stones fallen in a deep well. Binnie slowed and sank very quietly down on a step in the shadows at the top of the stairs. She could not tell from the voice whether the visitor had just arrived or was on the point of leaving, but she knew from the plummy tones that it was Quimby talking with her mother. She preferred to stay out of sight until she was certain that he was going or, better yet, gone.

Mrs. Howe's voice sounded as if she were coming out of the front room. Yes, they both stood now at the bottom of the stairs by the front door.

"They are evil, daughters of Satan," Quimby thundered like some angry prophet in the Bible who had discovered sin.

"Since the corporations take credit for all that is good in Lowell, including the high moral character of the girls, you should make that observation to those responsible for their being here, don't you think? Rather than to me? I simply give them lodging." Mama's voice was mild but her shoulders were rigid.

Quimby missed completely her sarcasm. "Which reminds me," he said. "You should have no one here who is not working now. The lodging is intended only for those who work for Merrimack, as you well know."

"How can my girls go in if there is no work? A weaver cannot make cloth out of air. She needs warp and weft to weave."

"Maybe so. But the leaders, those who were first to throw their bonnets into the air, those must be gone from here."

"They will be if and when they can collect their money. With all the women leaving, there has been a run on the bank. Our savings institution has no specie left to pay out on withdrawals. They've sent to Boston for more hard cash, I hear. The women want cash in hand just as you do. And now . . . ." Mrs. Howe moved to open the front door.

"Hear me, Mrs. Howe. As soon as possible, I want those creatures out. I shall be sending you newcomers to fill the beds."

"Oh, as to that, I should tell you. Best leave this house empty for a bit. We have some sickness. Besides,"—Mrs. Howe shook her head in an anxious way—"one of our girls is worrying so over her spots that . . . ."

Quimby did not let her finish. "Spots?" he asked. "Spots, did you say? We don't want any spreading. Keep to yourselves here then." He moved rapidly to the door, opening it himself. "See to it that she pays for a doctor's visit," he tossed over his shoulder as he hurried out like a man being nipped by a dog.

Binnie came down the stairs calling out, "What sickness, Mama? I hope you had your fingers crossed when you said that."

"Why it's no fib, Binnie," her mother said defensively. "I heard Mrs. Penfield coughing the other day."

"And the spots, Mama? The worrying spots?"

"That's not *exactly* a fib, either. Sarah's freckles have been worrying her terribly. All the lemon juice she has put on has not faded them one bit. And I never said a word claiming *she* was sick, did I?"

Binnie's eyes had widened as she listened. Hands on hips, her mother eyed her back as if daring Binnie to contradict her. They both broke in the same instant. Binnie guffawed while her mother whooped with great rolling gusts of laughter. Finally Binnie, clutching her aching sides, gave one last appreciative moan of laughter as her mother wiped stream-ing eyes with her apron.

"We needed that," Mrs. Howe declared.

On the next day, Binnie made only one trip out, to remind everybody of the rally planned for the day after. Maria prac-ticed her speech in the afternoon as Binnie listened carefully and suggested changes in the order and the words of some of the sentences.

Watching the restless, anxious crowd on the hill next to the Stone House Hotel, Binnie worried over how it would sound to others. Maria made a good appearance but Binnie wondered if her manner wasn't too aloof. She turned her at-tention back to the speech, which was half-finished already.

" . . . I tell you what they say is next to a lie. It is a myth of the manufacturing interests that capital and labor make *equal* partners. What kind of partnership is it when many labor mightily and long for the profit-loving pleasure of the few? They are making of us a lower class as surely as they raise themselves to a new aristocracy."

Binnie wished that Maria would not read so slowly. Her careful, precise reading drained the words of all feeling. She wished, too, that Maria would lift up her eyes from time to time and use her hands more. The next part was Binnie's fa-vorite and she tensed, waiting for the sentences that she had helped to shape.

"Our forefathers believed that all men are created free and equal. They fought the tyrannical British for their right to a free society, one without classes. We, their daughters, are no less a part of mankind. We, too, are created free and equal. But I ask you: How are you free if another takes a lien on your body and you work for a pittance? How are we—women and human beings—free if we must live as moles and bats with only a few precious hours of the night for our own lives?"

That did it. *Whoosh.* Binnie let out a great sigh of relief as she heard women shout "True, too true" and "Amen" in agreement. Maria looked up in surprise and paused. It was just long enough. The continuing response encouraged her to keep her head up as she worked her way to the ending.

". . . only those bound down in ignorance can believe and accept the myths of this new repressive aristocracy. We will fight on. These captains of industry may own the factories, the banks, the railroad—all the machinery of society—but they do not and *cannot* own us. Remember: We are the daughters of a great Republic and the daughters of the Sons of Liberty."

Maria's speech had just the effect Binnie had hoped for. After the cheers and clapping, woman after woman pushed her way to the front to add her testimony about the truth and justice of their cause. They spoke of the dictatorial control over every part of their lives, the physical abuses to health and safety, the unjust dismissals. Every speech confirmed the belief that the final goal was not simply money but rather freedom and equality, and every speech strengthened the determination to hold out.

Binnie sensed when the meeting was drawing to a close and wiggled her way to the front. At a signal, everybody on the hill linked arms and started down to sweep through the streets of Lowell once again. They sang louder than ever, "I will not be a slave. . . . I cannot be a slave." Someone made up a new chant and finally the whole procession was shouting: "Rescind! Rescind! Rescind! Give it back! Give it back! And we'll unpack!"

Binnie was a little confused as to what it was that should be given back. Their wages or control over their lives? No matter, they were entitled to both, she decided. Flushed and exhilarated, she didn't notice when the first egg hit. But when the second hit the shoulder of the woman in front of her, the foul smell of rotten egg jerked her out of her state of bliss. Over the determined singing of the women, she could hear now the yells and jeers. Startled, Binnie looked over her left shoulder.

A cluster of men stood on the corner by Wyman's Exchange. Some of them must have come just then from the Bleachery, for the sharp smell of the chemicals they worked with hung in the air. They carried, too, the India rubber garments that they used on the job.

"For shame, for shame!" a woman's voice scolded. Whatever else she said was drowned out by the men's catcalls of "Shameless women . . . . Hussies . . . ."

Binnie was determined not to cry and squinted hard to keep the tears locked in. Through watery eyes she saw the lean face of Boggs, the mean overseer from the Dye House. She felt certain that he had thrown the rotten egg. In a rush, the women rounded the corner. The main body broke up into splinters as they made for their separate boarding houses.

"What do we do now?" Binnie asked Maria that night.

"What do we do? Wait. We wait." She wore a grim expression as she said it.

By the end of the third week in October, more than 2,000

had become members of the Association. But the wait was taking its toll of their patience and their savings. More women left for home and their families. Only four boarders —Maria, Dorcas, the widow and Sarah of the freckles—were left at the Howes.

The widow Penfield had nowhere to go, no money to pay her board. Mrs. Howe, listening to the widow's stuttering explanations, came to an agreement with her. To pay her way, the widow helped out by doing the work that Mary Kate used to do and some of the mending. Dorcas Boomer found tailoring work that she could bring to the house and do. She put swift, savage stitches in the heavy canvas workingmen's trousers, stopping only occasionally to suck a pricked thumb and curse under her breath. Binnie read newspapers and ran errands with an uneasy hope that the leaders would find a way out of this swamp of inaction.

On a chilly, pinching day in the fourth week of October, Binnie came home to a shocking sight. The smart calfskin trunk sitting in the entry belonged to Maria Teasdale. Maria, who had said "wait" and had enough money to hold out, was leaving. Not through any choice of hers, she explained to Binnie. Her father had written, commanding her to come home to Maine.

"He says, besides, that he is sick and as his only daughter my place is there to nurse him," she said and fell silent. She chewed nervously on her lower lip and then burst out, "I think his illness is a hoax. His illness is fear, fear of what's happened in Lowell. Fear that his daughter might be one of those 'radical, rioting Amazons.'"

In her mind Binnie understood the logic and reason of Maria's leaving. But in her heart she felt betrayed. It was as if a torch had been lit but one by one people were refusing to carry it.

The look in Binnie's eyes must have stung Maria for she added, "I don't dare to *not* go, but I shall be quick to tell him the truth. Since I made that speech, I hear my name is at the top of the list at Merrimack and I'm *proud* of that. Anyway, the corporation will never forgive or take me back so I might as well be at home as here. Will you write to me, Binnie? I shall be anxious to hear a firsthand account of the outcome.

"What outcome?" asked Binnie bitterly. "One way or another this strike is virtually done for. And there was no point to anything that we did, no point to the fine speeches."

"Binnie, don't say that! The factories, the system is changing and not for the better. These things had to be said aloud. I and others may go, but the factories will be here for years to come. What you said, what you helped me to write will keep our sisters from being duped. Why, you were the very one who added such convincing words to my speech, the ones that proved we were right to turn out. You of all people can't believe that it was all for naught."

Binnie swallowed hard. She had nothing to say. Maria had not finished yet.

"You are too young and the older women would not have listened. But by rights you should have been up there before the crowd, not me. I don't have the feeling for it that you do . . . or leastways I can't make it so plain as you do. But you must, you must . . . ." Maria stopped and started again. She spoke fiercely as if to contradict her own words about lacking passion. "If I have learned anything from this experience, it's that we, women, must find the means, a way to make a better case for ourselves. Binnie, you have a good mind and a talent for expressing ideas. They are both gifts which you must cultivate and feed."

Maria's eyes were glistening, her smile tipped crookedly as she came to a halt. There was an awkward silence. She put a hand out and squeezed Binnie's shoulder. "Having seen the size of your appetite, Heaven knows I shouldn't be urging you to do any more feeding of any kind."

Both of them laughed at Maria's lame joke. They laughed longer and harder than it deserved. Then Binnie soberly promised to write Maria the news from Lowell.

There was no news to write. The days continued in exactly the same way: women leaving Lowell, women entering Lowell, the mills running haltingly, if at all, with half of their machinery idle.

Rumors swept through the ranks of women regularly. One said that the corporations had not kept a very exact record of all who had turned out. There would be no gigantic blacklist. It presented some of the hold-outs with the opportunity of returning to work. The very thought of this depressed Binnie and she hunted for a distraction.

She took her mother's scrapbook up to the attic and sat on Maria's bed to leaf through the pages. She found the account of that earlier strike and started reading. She read with horrified fascination, for every sentence, every word about that turn-out in 1834 sounded like a mocking echo.

". . . the reduction in the wages . . . caused much grumbling among the girls. . . . They struck . . . a procession was formed and they marched about town . . . ," said the Lowell *Journal.*

Even the ringing resolutions that they passed sounded the same. The only difference that Binnie could find between then and now was in the numbers. Eight hundred had walked out by the first of March in 1834. Two thousand had marched out this October. The first one had lasted less than one week; this one had endured four weeks already. The outcome of the earlier strike was the most upsetting part of the account. She read: ". . . most of the disaffected are returning to their work, ready to take a diminished price and continue to labor. . . ."

Binnie thought of all the women who must have left Lowell in 1834 rather than continue to labor at the diminished price. If only, she thought, everybody had stayed together instead of scattering about the countryside, they might have built something that couldn't be shaken off, a lasting union. Their very sense of worth and independent spirit had been their undoing. To be able to enter and leave the factory system at will was both a strength and a fatal weakness today as it had been then, Binnie thought sadly. They were doomed to repeat the cycle. And that thought was the end-all for her.

Binnie, who had followed the committee's lead with unquestioning loyalty and raced cheerfully about town all these last worrying weeks, could not bear it any longer. She sat unseeing, with the open book on her lap, and wept. Her tears were for all those who had seen the factories' promise of a workers' paradise and independence for themselves betrayed. She wept for the women who had left Lowell, then and now, and she wept for those who stayed. She cried for herself and even harder for her mother, whose loyalties were torn between the needs of her friends and the needs of her family. At last Binnie, drying her eyes, made up her mind and went downstairs. What she was doing might not make any difference, but she wouldn't stop because *not* doing was even more unsatisfactory.

There were fewer messages these days and Binnie carried them without that urgent sense of purpose that had brightened the earlier trips. She reminded herself that there were lulls in every battle and went doggedly about town.

She heard the news first not from any committee member but from her mother. There was no general announcement to the public at large. The strike, Mama said, had managed to achieve a small measure of success.

Quietly, very quietly, the Hamilton Corporation had rescinded the new rate of board for the operatives who were paid on a daily basis. And they were encouraging the return of their experienced hands. They needed the spinners and drawers too much to do otherwise. Finished cloth was fetching the highest prices ever in the marketplace and the mills were anxious to step up their production.

"Inasmuch as Merrimack, too, will be discontinuing the extra allowance," Mama said, "people are going back to work."

Binnie could not help thinking it was a sad, limping way to end the struggle which had begun with so much fervor.

"Quimby came by to say they'll take everybody back, everybody but the ringleaders and the officers of the Association. Most of those have left, anyway. I know you were among the first out but I don't think he'll hold it against you. What do you want to do? Do you want to go back? It's up to you."

Once again her mother had left a decision to her. This

time Binnie had a surer sense of her direction. "I will go back. But only until next summer's term. I mean to get more schooling. I'm not going to spend the rest of my life in a factory."

Binnie had no notion of what she would do when she was full grown. But she had learned one thing from the turn-out. Words were powerful tools. She wanted to acquire more of them and learn to use them with skill. She'd get not only more schooling but better schooling, she resolved.

"Mama, I want to keep the money I earn. I want to do more than common school. I want to go to high school, maybe even go away to the seminary, the Troy Seminary in New York state. Adam will have to look to his own tuition because I'll need my earnings for my own tuition."

The boldness of her words frightened her a little but she spoke them firmly. Mrs. Howe turned her back to Binnie as she moved to wipe her hands on a towel. They were deeply stained with walnut juice, for Binnie had gone nutting at Granny Anna's the day before. Binnie waited, but her mother said nothing.

She started again, "Mama . . . ."

Her mother interrupted her. "I'm glad," she said. Then, in a rare show of affection, Mrs. Howe leaned forward to give Binnie a kiss on the top of her head. Wordlessly, Binnie put up her arms and gave her mother a hard squeeze in return.

"Listen, Binnie. Adam is not your worry. He has more avenues for earning money than you do and he'll value his education all the more if he pays for it himself. It's never seemed right to me that you should work in the factory. And certainly not right that you should not have the benefit of money you earned yourself. It's only fair that you should

196

have an equal opportunity for learning. Anything less is unjust, unfair."

Her mother's last words bounced in Binnie's head. Was a passion for justice something that could be inherited? Like dark eyes or a straight nose? Maybe she had gotten her own sense of fairness from Mama just as she had gotten her straight brown hair from Papa? Binnie shut off the thought just in time to avoid an attack of embarrassed giggles.

"I'm going for a walk," she said and escaped.

She stood on the back step for a moment with an apple in her hand. She held the apple by the stem, turning it around and around very slowly as she murmured "A . . . B . . . C . . . ." Whatever letter the stem broke off at was the initial of your true love. It was very hard to get past *L*, she knew. She turned the apple another small fraction as she set off.

The fall wind that had sent such a rich harvest of nuts down from the trees nipped at her heels. It was a purifying wind, cleaning the streets of smells and sending dry leaves scattering ahead of her. She wanted to see if Packy had heard the news.

Yes, he already knew about the corporations' backing down. Did she know about the resolution of support that the National Trades' Union Convention had finally passed?

Both—the retreat and the resolution—seemed too little. Binnie was still nagged by a sense of failure. It would have been more satisfying to win bigger changes, more vigorous support. She and Packy argued over this as they strolled to the center of town.

"You want too much. Those men could have done worse at that convention. They could have ignored you all completely. After all, there are more workingmen for them to worry about than there are working women, you know. No, you're an ungrateful child, Miss Binnikins. Half a loaf is better than nothing." Packy smiled down at her.

That pesky boy had been growing, and faster than she. He was more than a couple of inches taller now and his shoulders had begun filling out to take the shape of a grown man. Binnie gave him a slow, searching look from the top of his head where the short, bristly hair was growing in to his bare feet.

"What a whale of an idea. Where have you been fishing for all that wisdom, Mr. Graybeard? In the China Seas?" She laughed at him.

His answering smile didn't last more than a second. He swore softly as he looked down the boardwalk.

"Holy Saint Colmcille and Columba, will you look at him now? He's half-seas over with drink."

Ahead of them on the walk was Boggs, the Englishman. He was talking to the air in the overly loud voice and blind way of a drunk.

"Where are they all now? Paradin' down the street so bold you'd think they owned the town." He snorted and swung his head to look around him. He had been leaning on a knobby gnarled stick. He lifted the stick and waved it in the air, almost unbalancing himself. "Send 'em around to me. I'll show them who's boss."

A woman coming toward him stepped off the boardwalk into the street to avoid him. He saw her and half-swung, half-lunged at her with the stick. It was as if he had meant to whack her, then changed his mind and tried to trip her. With a squeak of fear, the woman jumped sideways like a startled hare. He roared with laughter, spittle drooling down from the corners of his mouth.

Binnie's eyes narrowed. She spoke to Packy without looking at him. "Run," she said softly from the corner of her mouth. "*Now*," she added urgently and went off herself at a flying pace.

It took no more than a few seconds to come even with Boggs, whose back was turned to her. He was teetering on the curb of the boardwalk and looking down the street. Binnie slowed, veered slightly and ducked her head. She went straight at him, her lowered head catching him in the small of his back.

His feet shot out from under him, toes pointing straight up at Heaven. For all his size, he went up into the air like a feather. He came down with the flat, smacking sound of a stiff board and lay in the dusty street in stunned silence.

By then Binnie had reached the safety of the corner. Packy, who had made a late start behind her, leaned against the wall a foot short of where she had stopped. He was laughing too hard to move any farther. Binnie looked back at Boggs and started to laugh herself. Finally, Packy wiped the tears from his eyes and spoke.

"*Ooff*. What a sight! I'll never forget it. Binnie, you should have been where I was and seen him when he went. Just like a well-turned pancake!"

He pulled himself away from the wall and, in unspoken agreement, they continued their interrupted walk in silence. At the corner of Merrimack, where they usually parted, Packy spoke again.

"Did you ever see a hummingbird? They're the smallest

of all birds. Tiny. But they dart so fast and so fearlessly . . . .
Do you remember when you . . . .?" He seemed to be thinking out loud. Then, shaking his head in wonder, he looked
directly at her and said, "You're like that."

Binnie's eyes dropped in embarrassment but she was grinning. She knew he had been thinking of the fat farm boy
with the stick. She could almost taste the pleasure from
Packy's compliment at the back of her throat. It felt as sweet
as the last drop of honey from a piece of comb.

"I have to warn you about something though, Binnie," he
said in a solemn voice. "You'll have to change your ways."

Startled, Binnie's eyes flew back up to Packy's face. He
had that look of severity with the straight dark eyebrows
pulled together.

"Ladies—genuine, genteel Ladies—who have ambitions
to live in Big White Houses"—the exaggerated stress that he
gave each word told her he was teasing again—"ladies don't
go around butting men like billy goats."

Binnie bit the inside of her cheek to keep from laughing.
She answered him with equal solemnity. "Ladies who live in
Big White Houses are poor lonely souls. Or so I understand.
I wouldn't know about that. I'm just a Factory Girl."

"What d'ya know about that! I'm a simple workingman
myself. Shake on it, partner."

And in the middle of the dusty street, they bowed to one
another and shook hands.

ℰ➲Author's Note

Lowell, Massachusetts, occupies a special place in the history of America's change from a farming nation to one where industry and manufacturing provided fantastic profits and a new wealth not tied to the land.

Since British laws prevented export of textile machinery, Francis Cabot Lowell (the merchant for whom the city was named) drew on a photographic memory to build the first American power loom. He also created a new form of ownership, the modern corporation, which made available enormous sums of money to foster growth of the infant textile industry. In the thirty-two-foot drop of the Pawtucket Falls, his Boston associates found the power to run many looms. The farmlands of Chelmsford bordering the Concord and Merrimack rivers thus became the site of the first planned factory community in America. On September 1, 1823, the great water wheel of the Merrimack Corporation began to turn, and within six months bales of finished goods were being shipped to Boston.

To keep the machines running, the mills needed many hands. But men in this still young and thinly settled country had too many other and better opportunities for work. Moreover, Americans were prejudiced against factory work of any kind. As Nathan Appleton (one investor) wrote, Americans had heard that "operatives in the manufacturing cities of Europe were notoriously of the lowest character ... intelligence and morals." Many Americans believed that manufacturing itself was the evil which corrupted and degraded workers.

Francis Cabot Lowell overcame both of these obstacles. He tapped a new source for labor, the women of New England, and attracted them by establishing the boarding house system. The corporations built handsome brick houses and supplied women of good "moral" character to run them. In these houses, families could be sure that their women and girls would live safely, protected from vice.

Until this time women of New England had been chiefly "money-savers," who increased a family's wealth by managing their households economically. Now they welcomed with innocent eagerness the chance to become "money-earners." Flocking to Lowell, they stayed there an average of three to four years as they earned and saved set sums for a dowry, a parent's mortgage, a brother's college tuition or finery for themselves. A small number of children, ten to fifteen years old, also worked in the mills, generally at the lowest-paid unskilled jobs such as doffers and lapboys.

The women formed ties of friendship among themselves and created a community with outstanding cultural attractions. Despite a fourteen-hour workday, they attended and supported lectures, concerts and classes in everything from botany to German. Visitors came from afar to marvel at and afterward praise this showcase of industry. They were impressed by Lowell's fresh new buildings, its rural setting and the model workers who placed equal value on honest labor and higher education. By 1836 Lowell's fame had spread around the world, but already there were smudges and dark spots in the rosy picture.

The very success of the Lowell Experiment brought

about a startling change in twenty short years. Investors whose pockets had been plumped out with amazing profits formed still more corporations in other communities all over New England. They were always building additions to the existing mills as well. So much competition drove the prices of finished goods down, and to keep up their dividends, corporations increased their production. Stockholders, alarmed by the prospect of smaller profits, pressed agents to cut wages, the one cost that was totally within their control.

With stockholders draining off all possible cash, there was never enough money to make repairs or install new and more efficient machines. Older-model machines broke down often, took longer to produce fewer goods and cost more to run. Again investors saw no way to keep their high profits except by cutting wages still further.

By the 1840s, the workload for women had doubled: Operatives in New England worked fifteen minutes a day longer than they had in 1829, tended four looms at a time instead of two and *earned less money for it.*

In Lowell itself, open green spaces between the mills were filled with additions to existing buildings, semidetached boarding houses replaced by solid blocks of housing with a loss of light and air. Rooms that used to sleep six girls were choked with beds for ten and twelve.

Factory girls fought the wage cuts and struggled to win laws limiting the working day to ten hours. But they failed to stop the steady decline in pay and the worsening of their living conditions. Finally, the Yankee girls of New England stopped coming to the mills. Their places were taken chiefly by immigrants—Irish, French-Canadian, Greeks, Italians—who had no farms or village homes to retreat to in bad times, and by the second half of the nineteenth century, Lowell had become exactly like the despised and depressing manufacturing cities of Europe.

Many people are aware of this last chapter of the Industrial Revolution in the United States, but few are familiar with the earlier years and the opportunity they presented for women. Harriet Hanson Robinson's account of her life as a mill worker in Lowell, *Loom and Spindle* (Thomas Y. Crowell, 1898; reissued by Press Pacifica, 1976) is a neglected classic. Her story inspired this book.

All the historical figures named did visit or live in Lowell as described. My Howe family is, of course, a fiction as are Packy, Frenchy, Granny Anna, Quimby and all the boarders. Although I could find no evidence linking Elias Howe, the inventor of the sewing machine, with any Howes actually living in Lowell, he did work at the Machine Shop from 1835 to 1837. I could not resist "adopting" him as a distant cousin of Binnie's. Kirk Boott, a real person and agent for the Merrimack Corporation, toppled from his carriage in front of the Merrimack House and died of a stroke in 1837. All descriptions of buildings and place-names are taken from accounts written in that time, city directories and advertisements in those directories.

In describing the 1836 strike and reactions to it, I used newspaper articles from the autumn and winter of that year. I am indebted to Thomas Dublin's book, *Women at Work* (Columbia University Press, 1979), for the very specific figures on the turn-out and new facts about the final outcome. Although the women did parade through town and hold public rallies, the rally near Stone House is a fiction. Maria's speech at that rally is a composite of speeches made in turn-outs from a number of mills over the years 1834–1846.

Phrases such as "the bonds of sisterhood" and forms of address like "Sister" sound curiously modern but are drawn in fact from the factory girls' own writings. This *was* how they saw and thought of themselves. It is more than likely that the Lowell experience—which brought financial independence and the sharing of ideas with a wide cross-section of women—acted as seedtime for the flowering later in the nineteenth century of the woman's rights movement.

Other valuable books which I used are: Philip S. Foner's *The Factory Girls* (University of Illinois Press, 1977) and Hannah Josephson's *The Golden Threads* (Duell, Sloan & Pearce, 1949). They give much information on women in that time and on life in Lowell, as well as being a pleasure to read.

I especially thank Phyllis A. Larkin, whose steady hand and careful editing kept this book on course.

ABOUT THE AUTHOR

ATHENA V. LORD was born in Cohoes, New York, where water-powered mills like those in Lowell operated in the nineteenth century.

The idea for *A Spirit to Ride the Whirlwind* began, she says, when she read a nineteenth-century account of life and work "in that prototype of all mill towns, Lowell, Massachusetts," and "learned that new technology turned sleepy New England hamlets into bustling boom towns as raw and mushrooming as any western settlements. The thousands and thousands of Yankee girls who left their families and homes to work in the first planned factory town showed an adventurous spirit and courage that was the equal of any frontiersman's. Their inquiring minds profited from contact with one another and led them later into the forefront of labor movements and woman's rights. This early chapter in America's industrialization was an eye-opening discovery for me, one that I wanted to share."

Ms. Lord, a graduate of Vassar College, is also the author of *Pilot for Spaceship Earth*, a biography of R. Buckminster Fuller, which was selected as a "Notable Children's Trade Book in the Field of Social Studies." She and her husband have four children and live in Albany, New York.